a herd of tiny elephants

And Other Short Fictions
By
Stan Leventhal

BB

BANNED BOOKS
Austin, Texas

The following stories have been previously published:

"The Buddy System" — *The James White Review*
"Schoolmarm" — *Mandate*
"The Showdown" — *16 Tales*
"A Herd Of Tiny Elephants" — *Blueboy*
"The Bold Sailor" — *Shadows of Love*
"The Crystal Storm" — *Gaylactic Gayzette*
"Word Into World" & "Body Language" — *Exquisite Corpse*
"Telesex" — *No Apologies*
"The Star of David" — *Torso*

A BANNED BOOK

FIRST EDITION

Copyright © 1988
By Stan Leventhal

Published in the United States of America
By Edward-William Publishing Company
Number 231, P.O. Box 33280, Austin, Texas 78764

ISBN 0-934411-13-1

For their friendship, creativity, intelligence, and support, this book is dedicated, in memoriam, to:

David Acker
Fred Cantaloupe
Glenn Person
Richard Umans

Contents

The Buddy System

"Conventional wisdom tells us that it is foolish to write about writers because *real* people do not wish to read about them, and to write about gay people is one step away from insanity because *nobody* wants to read about them. Us. So, I decided my next novel must be about a gay writer."

"Of course," I said and knew that we were going to be friends.

"More coffee?"

Lawrence turned to look for the waitress. We had been introduced only twenty minutes before at the office of a magazine that occasionally published our work. I had read several of his stories, liked them, and was stunned and pleased that he knew of me and had a similar opinion. When he asked if I had time for a cup of coffee at the diner down the street I didn't hesitate. One meets so few writers that one really likes. Besides, I thought he was very handsome. For a moment I considered making a pass but decided not to. Even though I have been told that I'm not bad-looking I figured I was not in his league. And I didn't want to louse up a potential friendship. So we did in fact become friends. Buddies, actually. I recall one night when we were out together — very drunk, probably holding each other up — that we were accosted by a gossip columnist of some acquaintance. "Darlings!" he oozed and pecked us on the cheek. "Lawrence, Stu, are you two, gasp, an item?" Lawrence glanced at me. The spasm of his left eyelid told me that he was going to say something very nasty, so I motioned him to remain silent.

"Henry," I placed my arm around Lawrence's shoulders, "we are *buddies*. In the pool of literature, when the hunky lifeguard blows his whistle, we pause, seek each others' hand and stand to be counted."

1

"That was very good," said Lawrence.

"You boys are terribly wicked . . . that's probably why I love you so. Off now!" He pecked us again and, preening, strutted back into the crowd.

It was shortly thereafter that Lawrence met Keith.

☆ ☆ ☆

"The baths are not about *sex.* They're about fantasy."

"Come off it, Lawrence. You go to the baths to get your rocks off. When you want fantasy you usually head for a Spielberg movie or read something by Lovecraft."

"That's true," he sighed. "I suppose admitting that sex is the attraction spoils the fun."

"You were telling me about this guy you met."

"Yes, we had a wonderful night. I lost count of the eruptions but I'd be willing to bet there hasn't been so much lava since Vesuvius." I chuckled. "Anyway, he actually called the next night, that was Sunday, and we had, can you believe it, a date."

"Don't tell me you're in love."

"Of course, it's too soon to say anything, but what I'm feeling is not restricted to my crotch."

His name was Keith, and Lawrence described him as ". . . the perfect male. Designer pecs, great bod, boyish face, good skin. He knows who Gertrude Stein was, prefers Talking Heads to Puccini and leaves sweet messages with my answering service."

"What does he do?"

"*Everything.*"

"For a living."

"He's the regional marketing director for a food conglomerate."

"What does that mean?"

"When I find out, I'll fill you in."

Neither of us had a lover and I was glad that he'd finally met someone he liked. I can't deny, though, that I felt a twinge of envy. The problem was figuring out if it was because Lawrence had found someone while I was still very much on my own, or because someone aside from me had made him happy. I would be lying if I didn't admit my disappointment because he'd never been interested in anything other than my brain. I was eager for the companionship of another writer, however, and found it a great relief to have someone to call who would

2

agree that editors are spineless; publishers, goons; and the general reading public, mostly moronic.

But I was not having much luck meeting men. Perhaps because I look a lot younger than I am and always say what I'm thinking. The ones who cruise me usually assume that I'm still a kid and lose interest as soon as they realize that I have a mind and am not easily manipulated. The ones who might enjoy my company never give me a chance because they think I'm too young and have nothing interesting to say.

And I'm terrible at sustaining a relationship. Three weeks is a major accomplishment. When a miracle occurs and I actually arrive at that elusive state of "seeing someone," one of us inevitably turns the other off by being too aloof or too eager. The last time I was "seeing someone" I would agonize over how many days to wait and call after a date. And if too many or too few days went by before hearing from him, I'd fear that he wanted to use me at his convenience, or imprison me forever. Perhaps I evoked a similar response in them. It just never seemed to work out.

Lawrence was always very supportive and managed to convince me that most of the time the fault was in the other fellow. I remember once, though, when he chastised me for letting a good one get away.

"All right, Stu, you're avoiding the issue. What happened with the geology teacher/body-builder?"

"Nothing, I simply never returned his calls."

"Why?"

"Because I got tired of always having to go out to Brooklyn. He never came to my place even once."

"Didn't you think he was worth the trip?"

"Well, yes, but aren't you the one who said if I made it too easy for them they'd just take advantage of me? If I remember correctly you said, 'The trout that leaps into the fisherman's boat is always thrown back; such willingness always creates suspicion.' "

"Dammit, Stu, that's not the way I put it!"

"Maybe, but that's the way I remember it."

"Anyway," he paused, "will you come to dinner on Friday? You must meet Keith." They'd been dating for several months and I had avoided an introduction.

"If I must, then I shall."

☆ ☆ ☆

3

Keith proved to be a charmer. His curly brown hair, fetchingly unkempt, as if it had been dried by the wind after a swim, framed a gentle, yet masculine face. Quick with a smile, his large eyes possessed an innocence that seemed to whisper, "trust me."

I found it easy to relax with them. Lawrence was in a particularly joyous mood, so proud was he to show off his prize, and Keith, like a blank page that assumes the character of whoever is writing on it, could get along well with anyone. About half-way through the tortellini pesto, however, the conversation sagged. I attempted to shore it back up. "Lawrence, this is the best pasta you've ever prepared." He grinned. "So, Keith, Lawrence told me that you're not very keen on Puccini."

"Who?"

"Puccini!" said Lawrence, exasperated. "The opera composer." "Oh," said Keith with a laugh, "I don't like opera."

"I understand you like to read Gertrude Stein."

"Read?" he asked, unabashed. "Wasn't she the one who gave that recipe for hash brownies to Alice What's-Her-Name?"

"That's right," I said, suppressing the urge to scowl at Lawrence. But I was determined to salvage the conversation. "What's your favorite thing in the whole world?"

"You mean, besides sex and food?" I nodded. "Scuba diving!" he said and proceeded to tell me everything there is to know about it. He described the sensation of drifting under water, immersed in a rainbow-colored world of fish and coral. It was poetic, heartfelt and enchanting. I had mentally deducted a few points from my evaluation for Puccini and Stein, but added ten bonus points for his description of the silent, kaleidoscopic sea. Keith emerged from my scrutiny as a good catch for Lawrence, so I gave their relationship my tacit seal of approval.

I would occasionally join them for a movie or a play. At first I thought that they felt sorry for me and invited me along because I was without a soul mate. But I soon realized that they needed me as a shock absorber so as not to wear each other out. Although they seemed to get along splendidly in most respects, they required a buffer because of the difference in their interests.

If we went to an escapist movie and Lawrence enjoyed it, Keith would say something like, "See, it wasn't Shakespeare but you liked it! Right, Stu?"

And I would murmur something like, "Man can't live by Shakespeare alone."

If we went to see an avant-garde play and Keith didn't like it, Lawrence would say, "If you saw more intellectual plays you would learn to appreciate them. Right, Stu?"

And I'd mutter something like, "You know what they say, one man's meat . . ."

It reached the point where I started to feel like a mediator. I was used to Lawrence's calls seeking comfort. Keith, however, began to call me as well. "I know that Lawrence is your best friend and I really shouldn't have called, but, well, we had another fight," as if I hadn't already heard, "and I thought if I could talk it over with you it might help."

I was as helpful as I could be. They usually argued over something like the fact that they'd already had Chinese food that week and one of them wanted it again. This would escalate into shouting and harsh words. They would not talk for several days and then make up. I thought there was some underlying tension that caused these rifts but had no idea what it was until Lawrence confided that he suspected Keith was cheating.

"And you're not?" I chided.

"No! I haven't been with anyone else since we started seeing each other."

"Did you make some kind of blood pact?"

"Well, no."

"How can you be sure he *is* fooling around? You don't know for sure. You'll just have to trust him."

"I want to."

"Innocent until proven guilty. It's the American way."

"Stu, I'm aware that Keith calls you to talk and you've been so good to us, I just want to thank you for all your support. Without you to keep us on an even keel, we wouldn't have lasted this long."

"Nonsense."

"You're a real buddy."

☆ ☆ ☆

Lawrence completed his novel, *The Lavender Quill Conspiracy*, and his agent had no trouble placing it. Full of intrigue, romance and humor, I enjoyed reading it.

Dancing with some friends at the Anvil one night, I saw Keith in the backroom engaged in a ritual of non-verbal communication with someone other than Lawrence. I don't think he saw me. I kept quiet about it.

I was busily involved in an assignment for a national slick that required much research, in-depth interviews and critical analysis. I went out every night to have a drink and unwind. A conversation with a stranger would occasionally arise, but things rarely soared.

One night a met a nice guy. Marty. A carpenter. We exchanged small-talk for a while and he invited me to his apartment. Three dogs, Mandi, Sandi and Brandi, spaniels all, cavorted about like hyperactive children until Marty and I fell asleep. I awoke to find the creatures in bed with us, as though I'd been a part of some bestial orgy. I called a few days after and left a message on the answering machine thanking him for a nice night. He didn't return the call until three weeks later. He said that he had gonorrhea and suggested a visit to the clinic. I had, until then, managed to avoid contracting any sexually transmitted diseases. Angered at first, I eventually calmed down figuring that an imbalance had been corrected. I was long overdue. It was my turn. I made an appointment with my doctor.

Keith had gotten into the habit of dropping by my apartment unannounced. It started when Lawrence was preoccupied with the completion of his book and wanted no distractions. But it continued after things had returned to normal. We would chat, usually about movies or their latest spat. Once he brought me a book with beautiful color plates of saltwater tropical fish. If I ever had the desire to go scuba diving, he'd be glad to guide me along, he said.

The three of us attended the Holly Near-Ronnie Gilbert concert and our spirits were lifted so high, we left the auditorium with our arms around each other, Lawrence in the middle. We ran into Henry in the lobby. "Darlings!" Peck. Peck. Peck. "Is this a brazen attempt to revive the lost art of the ménage à trois?"

"Don't be silly," said Keith with a smile.

"Fuck you," said Lawrence, his eyelid beginning to squirm.

I pretended I hadn't heard the remark. "How are you, Henry, and what's the hot scoop?"

"Those rumors about Richard Gere and William Hurt, all *untrue.*

"That's a relief," I sighed.

"The rumors regarding a certain writer and his perfidious lover, however, are *very* true."

Lawrence's eyelid began to shimmy and Keith's jaw dropped to his knees.

"Henry," I pushed him aside, "words simply won't do. Onward," I said to my companions.

☆ ☆ ☆

I went to the doctor and was tested for gonorrhea. I was poked, scraped, given a prescription and told not to indulge for a few weeks. Going about my work, I began to notice a peculiar rash that itched like nothing I'd ever experienced. When I called for the results of my test—which turned out to be negative —I told the doctor about it and he suggested another examination.

"Do you have any pets?" he asked.

"No."

"Curious. I must inform you that you have a rather advanced case of scabies, which is usually gotten from animals."

So as blind luck would have it, I'd escaped infection from Marty, the carpenter, but Mandi, Sandi and Brandi had given me a souvenir of the encounter. Getting rid of the scabies was not easy, but I followed instructions until the every trace was gone. Thanks to the supposed gonorrhea, the reality of scabies and my own paranoia, I was kept out of the sexual arena for more than three months.

It was during the afternoon, on a Thursday as I recall, that Keith dropped by. I offered him a beer.

"I never kissed you on your birthday last month," he said as if he had to apologize.

"I wouldn't let *anyone* kiss me on my birthday this year, let's not go into the details."

"I'd like to make up for it now," he insisted. Loosening his tie, he walked over to where I sat. I turned my head, expecting a quick one on the cheek. He held my jaw, forced his tongue down my throat and rubbed my groin. It felt heavenly but I pulled away.

"Do you know what you're doing?"

"Yes," he said, unbuttoning my shirt.

"If Lawrence finds out about this he'll kill us both and commit suicide."

"Then let's make sure he never finds out." He winked. I'd gone without the touch of a man for too long to resist.

7

☆ ☆ ☆

Sex with Keith was a lot less than I ever would have imagined. He knew all of the appropriate maneuvers but after a few minutes I was so overcome with guilt that I divorced myself from the act and switched on my automatic pilot. Perhaps he felt guilty as well because when it was over I could tell that he wasn't any happier about it than I was. He left without another word passing between us.

Certain that our encounter would never get back to Lawrence, I forgot about it. I began work on my first novel and eased myself back into social activities. The first time I had dinner with Lawrence and Keith, I half-expected conspiratorial looks from Keith and suggestive remarks about treachery from Lawrence, but my fear was unnecessary. Lawrence's book was doing very well, critically and commercially. Keith had gotten a promotion. Everything was as smooth as possible.

One day, soon after that, Lawrence called and said that he had to see me right away. The degree of anger in his voice unsettled me; I was trembling when I answered the door. He waived the formalities with the palms of his hands and planted himself on my couch.

"The most important thing here is the truth. I've got to know. Keith told me something that I can't believe. Now I'm asking you. Did you and Keith ever sleep together?" I didn't know what to say so I didn't say anything. "You probably think I'll go haywire if you say 'yes'. But please, I'm begging you, the truth is what I'm after."

I had trouble getting the words out. "If you mean what you asked the answer is 'no'. We never slept together."

"Did you ever have sex?"

"Yes. Once." I felt like I was on trial; the anxiety while waiting for the verdict was killing me. Lawrence just sat there looking blank. I wanted to shout, "Hit me, hate me, tell me that you never want to talk to me again, but please, please end this torment." I couldn't say it. The best I could manage was, "Why did Keith tell you?"

"Because he wanted to hurt me. He told me that he seduced you right here on this couch about two weeks ago."

"It's true."

"But I didn't believe him. So he said that the two of you had been getting it on behind my back for a long time. I knew one of his statements had to be false. You're not going to believe this, Stu, but I could have handled it. I mean, he was

8

fucking everyone in sight. But when I realized that he'd lied, just to hurt me, I told him it was over."

"Is it over between us too?"

"It doesn't have to be." He moved closer.

"You don't hate me?"

"I'll never hate you. But there's only one way to make amends." I was greatly relieved. "What's that?"

"Can I fix us a drink?"

"Of course," I said.

He filled two snifters with brandy and we toasted silently. Placing his hand on my knee he said, "I want what Keith got."

I almost choked, then giggled. "You're joking. You don't mean . . ."

"Yes I do." He drained his glass and removed his shoes.

"You're serious?"

"Uh huh." He nodded and began to unbutton his shirt. "I never thought you were interested," I said softly. He stopped and looked up. "I thought I wasn't good enough for you."

"I can't believe this," I confessed, "I thought that I wasn't good enough for *you!*"

Our eyes met and fused into a single vision. We stared at each other. It lasted a moment but seemed longer. Leaning forward, our lips came together; we tasted each other slowly. I unbuckled his belt and then my own.

☆ ☆ ☆

My first novel, *Ménage*, centered on the shifting relationships of three gay men. Published by a small press, it garnered some complimentary critiques from serious literary types and sank like a barbell. Lawrence's novel was nominated for the Endicott Award for Suspense Fiction.

We moved in together. A large loft in Tribeca with a panoramic view of lower Manhattan and the Jersey coast. Lawrence said that he wanted to adopt a puppy but I managed to talk him out of it. He settled for a tank of saltwater tropical fish.

In his weekly column, Henry wrote, "Two up-and-coming authors have tied the matrimonial typewriter ribbon and have set up word processing in a spiffy downtown loft, certain to be the scene of this years' most delectable literary soirees."

I thought that finding a lover and settling down would solve all my problems. Silly me. Everyone warned us that two writers could never live together because rivalry would create too much tension. That's not the case, however; Lawrence and I are still supportive of each others' work and we share all of our triumphs and defeats. I guess that's possible when friends become lovers.

But in our zeal to achieve greatness, or at least, goodness, we have become very critical and protective of each others' mental activity. He gives me a hard time because I prefer Ellington to Wagner. And I have to admit I berate him on occasion for spending too much time with Agatha Christie when he should be reading Tolstoy.

And the jealousies. We chose to establish a monogamous relationship and as far as I know, we've succeeded. I've been faithful, though at times I almost crossed that line. And Lawrence says that he hasn't strayed either. But ever since we started living together the temptations have multiplied. When I used to go out I was usually ignored. Now I find myself having to reject a lot of attractive offers. Lawrence is experiencing the same thing. Ironically, since we're no longer available to the cruising public, we're very much in demand. When we go out together it's very flattering. If one of us is out alone, however, the other can't help wondering whether he's succumbed to a flirtation.

It's not easy to be someone's lover and buddy. Both of us will readily testify. The only thing we really fight over, though, is the word processor. We're both gluttons when it comes to monopolizing it. So, after much deliberation we decided to order another. It should arrive any day.

Tax-Free

Sometimes it's the garbage trucks, sometimes the drunks. The early morning noises that explode on the street just over his windowsill wake him up every day. Unless he's been hired for an all-nighter. Usually he's in bed by three and up at around eight. When the weather is so cold that his window is shut and caulked, the street sounds are muffled, but they still wake him up. He lies in bed, unable to slide back into dreaming, unwilling to leave the security of his mattress on the floor.

Every morning he has about two hours of "free association" time, a phrase he picked up from a movie he sat through twice. He replays the highlights of recent events or puzzles over the strangeness of a recurring dream. In the most frequent one, he wins an award—a gold statuette—and sees himself in a tuxedo, ascending a small flight of stairs to a stage with a podium. An enormous audience of faceless people screams and applauds as he leans into the microphone and thanks them for taking notice of him. He awakens feeling good all over. In another, he's hiding in the cabinet beneath the kitchen sink, praying that his parents and teachers—who are ransacking the house—won't discover his whereabouts. This dream always leaves him with a sense of fright. He awakens wondering why they are looking for him; the dream always ends before he can find out.

His cock, always at its hardest in the morning, beckons his hands or commands a roll-over so that it can be wedged tightly between his stomach and the hard mattress. Sometimes ho'll cum like this, picturing himself in an auditorium clutching a microphone, moaning and sweating, hips shaking at the eager young faces that hover at the edge of the stage.

11

He goes to the bathroom and checks his face before pissing and showering. His skin is usually pretty clear, except sometimes a pimple will appear on his forehead due to a hair clogging up a pore. He curses and slams his fist down on the sink. All day long he washes it and checks it out in mirrors wherever he is to see if it's grown or shrunk. If the pimple seems unusually large, he hides himself in movie theaters near Times Square. Slasher films, as some people call them, are what attracts him lately. He fondly remembers the scene in *Mother's Day* when the victim, presumed dead, stabs the bad guy in the back with an electric carving knife. The blood, so much more colorful and abundant than in real life, splattered all over the screen leaving permanent stains in his memory. When he saw that scene for the first time, his cock snapped to attention. Now all he has to do is replay the scene on the monitor in his brain. His cock stiffens and doubles in size before the bad guy keels over, the knife still vibrating, buzzing like the drills that tear up the streets. Afterwards, he wonders what it would be like to die. He pictures cartoon versions of heaven and hell, with angels strumming lyres or devils with pitchforks. He can think of hundreds of reasons why he should end up in each place. When he balances his good and bad deeds, they cancel each other out in a one-to-one correspondence. He figures it could go either way. He'd prefer to be with the smiling angels, but he's prepared to accept the devil's anger. He did, after all, run away from home.

He smokes a joint while sipping his morning coffee, light and sweet, while the small black and white television set — at least fifteen years old — he figures silently thrusts flickering images at his face. The coffee mug empty, another roach in the ashtray, he listens to a record on the small, portable stereo with fuzzy-sounding speakers. One of the four albums he owns, all lifted from a secondhand record store, is a two-disc set by Bob Dylan. "Absolutely Sweet Marie" is his favorite song. "Your railroad gate, you know I just can't jump it/sometimes it gets so *hard*, you see," he sings along in a voice that is higher and less cracked than Dylan's.

In the early afternoons he occasionally goes to the bars. All over town they fill up with businessmen and as yet undiscovered artists who take lunch hours that frequently don't require food and often last longer than sixty minutes. He orders a club soda and manages to strike a deal before having three sips and lighting a cigarette. His customers are usually younger

12

and better-looking than the ones he gets through the escort services. And they don't ask him a lot of questions or show him photographs of their families. It's strictly wham-bam-thank-you-Sam and then they go back to their offices. A blow-job is ten dollars. He finds a suitable spot nearby at no extra charge. To fuck will cost twenty-five dollars plus hotel fee or fifty dollars at his place. For kissing, add another twenty-five. He can easily clear fifty dollars per afternoon on his own and at least a hundred any night by putting himself on call with one of the escort services that he is registered with.

The man on the telephone gives him the name of a hotel and a room number. Then says, "Pretend you're a college student," or "I told him you're interested in sports." He journeys to the hotel and knocks on the numbered door. It's usually opened by a heavier, older guy. "I'm a college student working my way through school," are his first words. Or, "I'm really into sports, 'specially baseball." He gets paid before he takes his clothes off. And usually gets a good tip while putting them back on.

There's a lot to be said for the "three-day work week," a phrase he learned from from his ex-friend Billy. They'd go to movies together, smoke joints, talk about their customers. Once they were hired to have sex together while someone watched. Afterwards they promised that they'd never do it together again unless someone paid them. One time they were hanging out at the bar on 9th Avenue and Billy accused him of trying to steal a customer. Billy punched him in the stomach. Then pulled out a knife and cut his arm. The sight of his own blood terrified him. He ran home and didn't leave his room for three days. It wasn't a very deep cut, but it took months for the scar to become almost invisible. He wore long sleeve shirts until you had to put your eyes right next to it to see it. Now his only friend is Ken, the bartender. Sometimes he gives him free drinks. When he sees Billy, they pretend they don't know one another. They pass quickly without any sign of recognition.

Always home by around six o'clock, he showers and, every two or three days, calls in. The television, with the volume turned up now, shouts a list of news events at him. He shakes his head when he hears something about the value of the dollar decreasing. He's afraid that he will have to lower his rates and his tips will lessen. That would mean more working hours and less time for himself. Hostage situations can make him put down his fork. He pictures Arabs with machine guns, splattering the walls of tents in the desert with the blood of American women and children. After the news, he prepares dinner. His favorite food is Kraft macaroni and cheese. It's fast and easy to make, fun to eat. He lets the taste linger in his mouth before rinsing it away with Coke or Pepsi.

Reruns of old comedy shows—like *Laverne & Shirley, Gilligan's Island,* and *Three's Company*—help the time move along while he waits for the telephone to ring. Smoking another joint, his memory replays tapes of incidents from his childhood and years at school. He can never control these thoughts; they seem to have a rotation all their own.

Laverne comes in with a bag of groceries and he recalls going to the supermarket with Mom, when he was young enough to ride in the shopping cart. She'd hand him boxes of cereal, cans of beans, cartons of milk and he'd arrange it all very neatly against the sides. As the wall of food grew up around him, he'd imagine himself in a fort, fighting off the Indians. When they'd get home Mom would say, "Good boys always wash their hands and face after hard work," and he'd run to the bathroom, work up a lather between his palms, scrub his face clean, then run to the kitchen and announce that he was a good boy.

Gilligan is on the beach with the Skipper and he remembers going to Virginia Beach with Dad. They'd wade out to where it was waist deep and he'd leap from his father's shoulders into the salty water. Then they'd swim out to the orange buoy and race back to the wet sand. Dad would buy him hot dogs with lots of mustard, soda pop, and allow him a sip or two of beer. "But don't tell your mother," he'd warn him.

Jack comes out of the bathroom with a towel around his waist and he thinks of Coach Sebretski, who hated him because he refused to shower with the other boys after gym class. The first time he took off all of his clothes and headed for the shower room, they'd looked down at their own hairlessness and pointed to the wiry bush sprouting from his crotch, laughing and joking. After that, he'd dress while they showered. One of the other boys, usually Drew, would go to the Coach and rat on him. The Coach would storm into the locker room and demand that he strip and shower. He'd refuse. They'd argue. And he'd always need a late pass for American History. When he thinks of Coach Sebretski, he always remembers Miss Parkins, his third grade teacher, the best he ever had. She was nice. And she said that he was the most handsome boy in the class. He thought that Todd was the most handsome boy in the class but didn't want to argue with her because he liked her so much.

When he thinks about the past, the thing that stands out most of all is the day he ran away for good. Mom and Dad barged into his room while he lay on his bed, naked, playing with his cock. They yelled at him; told him that he was evil, hell-bound for sure. They locked him in his room. He busted the window and escaped with a knapsack full of clothing and some *Silver Surfer* comics. On the turnpike, his thumb stuck out, he hitched a ride north with a fat, smelly trucker. He arrived in New York and stumbled around until a skinny Puerto Rican kid started talking to him; told him how to get to the Port Authority building and how he could earn easy money there.

The telephone jerks him back to his room and the cackling television. He turns it off and answers the phone, reaching for his pad and pen so he can write down the necessary information: which hotel, the room number, and who he's supposed to pretend he is.

He showers again and carefully selects what he thinks the customer will like. It's usually the same pair of snug jeans with one of his dozen or so white t-shirts. He makes sure that he has a few imported rubbers and recalls the first time a customer insisted that he use them. "Haven't you heard about the health crisis?" asked the heavy-set, jowly man with glasses. He didn't want to admit that he hadn't so he said, "Sure." Lately, it seems that all that Ken, the bartender, wants to talk about is the health crisis. He'll never forget the first time he stretched the sheath of latex over his cock. It felt good. Like a delicate hand caressing him, making him harder.

A hotel room with the shades drawn, a large bed, the lights dim, is where he finally finds himself. More often, the better ones and not the flophouses he occasionally endures. Most of the time the customers are fat and over fifty. They have uncommonly large cocks that he can barely get his mouth around, but accommodation in his deceptively small ass is no problem. Many of them pull out pictures of their wives and children to show him. He can't understand why they think he wants to see the pictures, or why they need his ass if they have a wife at home. But he gets fifty dollars an hour, two hundred and fifty for an all-nighter, tips and there's no extra charge for kissing. He can earn over a hundred dollars a day, almost any day he chooses. Tax-free. Pretty good, he thinks; no one that he knows can do as well.

15

He returns home and clicks the light on. Strips and looks at himself in the mirror. His body is still hard and slim, his face boyish with green eyes and parentheses around his mouth when he smiles. His hair is straight, the color of wheat and almost touches his shoulders. He turns and looks at himself from several angles. Grabs his cock like a microphone and poses. He turns off the light and plops onto the mattress, covering himself with the blanket. On his side, he brings his knees up to his chest, clutches the pillow with his left arm and closes his eyes. He hopes that he will dream about the gold statuette and adoring audience. He prays that he'll spend eternity with the smiling, musical angels and not the silent, smirking devil.

The Showdown

When Walker asked if I wanted to go to the jack-off finals I hesitated because it was, after all, a Friday night and I couldn't stand the thought of missing an episode of *Miami Vice*. Watching Don Johnson in action while massaging my cock was my usual activity on Friday nights between ten and eleven.

"I have plans for Friday night."

"Look," said Walker, "the contest doesn't start until midnight. You can jerk yourself off and have plenty of time to shower and meet me so we can see some real pros at work."

"Do people really jerk off professionally?" I asked, giggling.

"At the Dungeon they do. The winner of the tournament gets five hundred dollars in cash and a round trip ticket to Key West."

After my Friday night ritual I met Walker. We had a beer and then made our way to the Dungeon, located in the heart of the meat packing district of the West Village. A black door with the address and the word "private" is the only indication that one has arrived at the right destination. Beyond the beaded curtain which separates the club from the reception area is a staircase that descends to the darkly-lit main area. Low-ceilinged with gray concrete walls, the rectangular room boasted a rack, guillotine and stocks. Other instruments of torture hung on the walls illuminated by indirect red lights.

Standing around the perimeter of the room were a variety of guys—young and old, fat and thin—all waiting with anticipation as the master of ceremonies checked the masking tape that marked the area for the contest. An oblong of about eight feet by four feet had been created with a gauge indicating feet and inches. The two contestants were to stand opposite

17

each other with toes touching — but not going beyond — two parallel red strips which were set about five feet apart.

The loud music which had been pummeling everyone's eardrums suddenly stopped and a handsome Hispanic man with a clipboard strode to the center of the floor and opened his arms in a gesture of welcome.

"That's Carlos Ramirez," said Walker, "he's the manager of the club."

"Men and boys, friends, fiends and fun-lovers," said Carlos, "this is the final round in the First Annual Dungeon Jack-Off Classic." Scattered applause emanated from various sectors of the club. "As those of you who have been with us from the beginning are aware, the finalists have demonstrated their extraordinary abilities in their previous bouts, and tonight they face each other to compete for the coveted prize."

"Let's get to the action," someone yelled.

Walker nudged me and whispered, "That guy lost last week by an inch and a half."

"Too bad," I sympathized.

"And now for the contestants," bellowed Carlos. "To my right, weighing one hundred and ninety-five pounds, from Scranton, Pennsylvania, Geoff 'Powerman' Morganstern!"

The spectators applauded as a strapping blond man with beard, moustache and diamond stud in his left earlobe, sauntered to the center of the room. He tore off his white t-shirt, pulled down the black 501s and gingerly stepped out of his pissburnt jockstrap. He twirled it on his index finger and tossed it into the crowd. A knot of onlookers jostled to claim it. The competitor flexed his bulging arms and jiggled his pectorals, strutting around the oblong, flaunting his mightily developed torso, narrow hips and enormous thighs. His cock, long and limp, sprouted from a mass of wiry bronze hair and his low-hanging balls swayed with his swagger.

"And his opponent," intoned Carlos, "from Eau Claire, Wisconsin, weighing one hundred and fifty-two pounds, Al 'Monster Dick' McKenna!"

Dark and lean, the other contestant slowly walked into the competition area pulling off his football jersey. He unzipped the bleached jeans and they fell to his feet revealing a well-defined stomach, perfect ass and sinewy legs. His thick cock hung to mid-thigh and would not have looked out of place on a man twice his size.

"You gentlemen know the rules," said Carlos, smiling. "Lubrication!" he commanded and a lovely young man appeared with a can of Crisco. He approached each contestant and spooned out a handful. They began application to their dangling cocks.

"All right. I'm going to start the countdown to the showdown. Five, four, three, two, one — GO!"

The athletes began stroking themselves. "Monster Dick" McKenna's organ responded first. It stood out perpendicularly, his dark shaft reflecting the light in all directions. It grew to approximately eleven inches as his scrotum tightened and his thighs began to quiver. "Powerman" Morganstern grimaced as his cock began to elongate, the balls of his feet pivoting on the floor. The rapidity of his pumping caused sweat to appear on his face as his nipples hardened, pointing slightly down and out.

The audience began to root and cheer.

"Go 'Monster Dick'," someone shrieked.

"Cream 'im 'Powerman'," screeched a fan.

The contestants eyed each other and increased the speed of their pulling. Sweat began to drip from all over their bodies. The golden down on Morganstern's buttocks caught the light as his meaty buns bounced up and down. The lean butt of McKenna, hard and well-rounded, remained firm and moved in tandem with the jerking of his hips.

Suddenly "Powerman" Morganstern started to groan and his body shook as his eyes disappeared into his head. He let out a low growl and his entire body vibrated as he let loose a jet stream that landed about a foot and a half from his toes. "Monster Dick" McKenna glanced at the floor and smirked. He began to thrust his hips to and fro, increasing the speed of his strokes. A high-pitched moan arose from his throat. As his back arched he shot a huge gob that landed right between Morganstern's feet.

The crowd was jumping and screaming as Carlos entered the oblong and raised McKenna's dry hand in victory. The two competitors shook hands as the various audience members began to disrobe, summon the Crisco boy, and enjoy for themselves the pleasure they had just witnessed.

"Let's go," said Walker.

"Are you kidding? The evening's just started."

"I was hoping you'd say that," he grinned.

We stripped, greased ourselves with Crisco and spent the next couple of hours testing our distance and stamina.

Orange Sunshine, Purple Rain

There is only one way for me to measure the success of a sexual encounter, and it has nothing to do with the intensity of the orgasm. Some are light and fast, others long and fierce, but I'm not sure what variables determine this. My mind, however, is the perfect indicator. If the only thing in the region of my conscious thought is the sexual play at hand, I have achieved the sought-after escape that signals success. If, however, my thoughts roam around, touching on memories or anticipations, then I know that sex, in spite of the orgasm, has not diverted me sufficiently.

Am I having fun? I ask myself.

Could be better, I reply.

Which is how I know that the scene I'm experiencing right now is devoid of everything except a sense of duty; that is to get through this without hurting my partner's feelings. My partner being Dennis Michael Walker, my ex-lover. He's working me with his mouth as I think of this, while Prince sings "Purple Rain" in the background. I'll probably explode at the proper moment and he will think that he has conquered me again. But it's only a chemical reaction. My body must defer to nature. Reason does not signify. But my mind remains independent and I can't stop thinking of my boyfriend in New York, or my parents, who live about thirty-five miles from here. Here is Dennis Michael's apartment.

He's looking at me now. Smiling. Flashing that goofy grin that asks: aren't I terrific? Don't I do it great? I smile back. I don't want to hurt his feelings, ruin his evening. But just before I offered my phony approval, I had been thinking about Tim, the man I met four months ago. The man in New York who I miss so much while I'm on vacation in Florida. Visiting my folks. But I haven't told them about Tim yet. It's too soon. You never know how long these things will last.

I met Tim—in a bar, of course—and we talked for a long time before deciding to go to my apartment for sex. Safe sex. An expression I didn't have to explain. It was understood that we would use condoms and refrain from the kinds of things we'd both done a million times before without a moment's hesitation. Licking ass. Swallowing cum. We had a wonderful time and began to get together about three nights a week. Eventually, we'd meet for dinner or a film and gradually crossed the line that separates the fuck-buddies from the boyfriends. And condoms—the straight man's defense against fatherhood—became a mandatory accessory for our activities.

When Dennis Michael and I were both naked I produced two condoms. I demonstrated my agility with them and he looked at me sourly. "You're kidding."

"Nope. It's the rage in New York. For anyone who wants to see the far side of thirty-five."

"Just 'cause some guys died?"

"That's reason enough for us."

"We Floridians don't think about that kind of stuff."

"Maybe it's time you started. You're taking a big risk just having sex with me, you know. This is for your own good."

He grudgingly slipped the other one on and modeled it, something I would have enjoyed more if he hadn't let his body go. What used to be firm and sleek was now soft and loose. He's still attractive. Such a youthful face. A bit chunky, though. And still a little slow in the snappy conversation department. We hadn't seen each other in a year and when I asked how he was doing, he replied, "Great."

"What's new?"

"Nothing."

When I ask Tim what's new, he can go on for two hours. At first I thought I was just fascinated by his work. He's a theatrical set designer and he knows lots of interesting people and hears all kinds of funny stories. I'm never bored for a moment. But Dennis Michael is different. A man of few words who never uses more than one at a time—unless he has to—and so tired of his job that he has to remind himself what he does.

"So, how's work?"

He thought about it for a while. "Okay."

21

I didn't press it, but I wanted to talk. It seemed like the logical thing to do, considering that we were sitting together with a table between us. I started telling him that I haven't yet overcome all the obstacles in the way of a fledgling singer-songwriter, "...so I've gotten four more songs published, but the record companies are still doing their damndest to pretend I don't exist."

"Gee."

"I guess I'm in kind of a malaise."

"Yup."

I'd be willing to bet that Dennis Michael has no idea what that means, but is too cowardly to ask. When I'd used that line on Tim, he smiled and said, "Well, I'll spread mayonn*aise* all over your mal*aise* and lick it off from now 'til dawn."

It's that kind of stuff that makes Tim so endearing. And I try to remember what was so attractive about Dennis Michael when we were lovers. He was cute. Beautiful, actually. But no personality. Back then I wasn't too big on personality, just looks. Guess I've come a long way.

But now it's time to get this over with. If I concentrate on Dennis Michael nothing happens. Zero. But I think about Tim's blue-gray eyes, his sense of humor, and that helps me enter phase two. And picturing Tim's firm, meaty ass and tapered thighs moves me into phase three. Pressure's building. I recall the sound of Tim's laughter in my ear and I'm soaring, holding onto the headboard now. Just a few seconds more. And there it is, faster than sound, moving like a wet torpedo. Droplets now. A calmness overtakes me as I'm emptied of all tension and strain. Thank you, Tim. Fuck you, Dennis Michael.

"How are your parents?" he asks.

"Fine," I say, wondering why he didn't ask during one of the long silences that joined us at dinner. Oh, now I see. He doesn't really want to know how my parents are. This is his way of indicating that it's my turn to service him.

We switch positions and I begin to work him over. It does not require much effort. I know this man's body. The original parts, anyway, not the new additions. Besides, I've had a lot of practice. This is easier than getting drunk and passing out. I wonder if Tim is fooling around in New York while I'm getting it on down here. We haven't signed any papers or drawn any parameters. Yet. The only thing that's been discussed and decided is that safe sex is the *only* sex. For now, anyway.

22

"These goddamn rubbers spoil the fun," says Dennis Michael. If my mouth were not otherwise occupied I would tell him that the distance between fun and death grows smaller every day. But that's too abstract for him. So I just chow down with more force. He groans. That ought to hold him for a while. God, but this is boring. Why do I get such a kick out of this with Tim? I used to enjoy this with Dennis Michael, but it's not the same. Everything's changed since I met Tim. Dear Tim. What will I pick up for Tim as a souvenir? A t-shirt that says Beach Bum? A sack of oranges? A Welcome To Fort Lauderdale piggy bank? The possibilities are astonishing.

He groans again. Or was that a moan? It's getting harder to tell. But at least he's responding. Perhaps to the acid? I can't believe people still *do* acid. I thought that went out with the Strawberry Alarm Clock. Are the Grateful Dead still together? I lose track. Time is so elusive. Thinking of time, I can probably be back to watch the 11:00 news with Mom and Dad. Who are sitting at home this very moment knowing that I'm having sex with Dennis Michael. They are too good to be true.

When I told them I'm gay I was prepared for the possibility that they might disown me. Or murder me on the spot. But Dad said, "I always suspected."

What a relief. Then I told Mom.

"It'll kill your father."

"No it won't. He already knows and he just played eighteen holes."

As soon as Mom had talked to Dad and realized he wasn't going to have a heart attack over it, she accepted me and my preference without reservation. Once a year I leave the winter of New York to visit Mom and Dad in sunny Fort Lauderdale. At night, when I'm going out they both say, "Have a good time." The next morning they ask, "Did you have a good time?"

"Yes."

"Did you meet anyone interesting?"

"Yes."

"What's his name?"

Just hearing them use masculine pronouns when enquiring about my evenings makes my heart jump up and down with joy. It was worth the risk of telling them my secret. They are an endless source of love. Last night, when I casually mentioned that I wouldn't be home for dinner tonight, Mom asked, "Got a date?"

I nodded.

"Anyone we know?" asked Dad.

"Dennis Michael Walker."

"The geometry teacher," said Mom, "the one who moved down from New York a few years ago."

"Right," I said.

"Your annual date," said Dad.

"Yes."

Then Mom said, "You've heard about this AIDS thing?"

I nodded.

"And you're taking all the necessary precautions?" added Dad.

"Yes."

"Have a good time," they said.

The fact is, I wasn't *that* eager to see Dennis Michael again. But he's the only person I know in Florida who's under sixty-five years old. So when I arrived I called to see if he wanted to get together—just for dinner and dancing. He said he couldn't wait. That was Monday. Today is Friday. And his cock is in my mouth. He appears to be writhing a bit. Good for him.

Dinner was fine. A place called the English Pub. After we'd established that I'm still working at the factory, performing on weekends, shopping demo tapes around, and that he's still teaching suburban brats how to slice up circles and sub-divide angles, the conversation simply stopped. I brought up all the recent national and international headlines I could think of, but he had nothing to say about anything. Maybe he spends too much time in the sun? Perhaps he's taken a few too many acid trips? It's probably just that he's so good-looking he can get whatever he wants without trying too hard. Like all human ornaments. The brains turn into oatmeal through lack of use. But they can't help it. No one is held accountable for their genes.

After dinner he took me to some disco. I forgot the name already.

"Do you wanna drop some acid?"

"No. Thanks."

He swallowed a hit and we started dancing. After six songs I drove us back to his apartment. And here we are shedding sweat onto his designer sheets.

Acid! I couldn't believe it. I haven't done any in about ten years. There was a time when orange sunshine was my favorite thing in the world, and I would trip out a couple of times a week. But that was when I was a kid. Then it didn't matter if I wandered around in a daze for forty-eight hours after coming down. These days I have responsibilities. A job to hold onto and a career to build. And even though I'm on vacation, I've still got to get back to my folks' place with me and their car intact. This ain't New York. Can't just hail a cab.

He groans again, but that might be because the stereo just clicked off. Thank God. It's not that I don't like Prince. It's just that "Purple Rain" is one of those songs that I heard several million times too many on the radio at work. And now I've just heard the entire album. Not bad. But not my idea of ideal fucking music. I prefer instrumental stuff. Vocalists are too distracting.

Was that a groan or a moan? I remember when Dennis Michael could come before my jaw muscles loosened up. He sure is taking his time. Maybe it's the acid? Or that he's getting older? Perhaps he needs the voice of Prince to keep him in the proper frame of mind? Should I turn the record over? As I recall, he used to get excited when I squeezed his nipples. I'll give it a try. There he goes. Here it comes. He's smiling. Breathing fast and hard. I guess I did all right.

"Would you turn the record over, please?"

"Sure," I say and get up to do it.

"That was great. Haven't lost the old touch, have you?"

"Guess not."

I lay down alongside, resting my head on his chest. I wonder what Tim is doing right now.

"You know, these rubbers aren't so bad. Takes some adjusting, though. Still, I could never get used to them on a regular basis."

"You just might have to, at some point."

"Humpf," he says.

I smooth down his hair.

"Have you been seeing anyone?" he asks.

"Yeah. Sort of. It's been about four months."

"What's his name?"

"Tim. And you? Seeing anyone?"

"Anyone I want."

"And what about love?"

"Love wasn't made for guys like us. I'm too particular and you're too romantic. I like it that we get together once a year and fuck. Gives me something to look forward to."

25

Did he always get this chatty after sex, or is it the speed in the acid? I'm not sure. Maybe next year at this time I'll still be seeing Tim and he'll come to Florida with me and I won't have to see Dennis Michael. That would be great. Because the question that's been straining for recognition in the back of my mind is growing more insistent. Ever since we got down to sex I've been afraid to focus my inner ear in that direction. But I can't ignore it for another moment.

Do I ever want to have sex — safe or any other kind — with Dennis Michael again?

No.

How should I tell him?

Don't tell him.

But when he finally figures it out — say two or three years from now — it might hurt his feelings. What then?

He'll get over it. Eventually.

Schoolmarm

The usual afternoon crowd gathered in Ruby Rae's Saloon. Because the sun was high and the dust had parched everyone's throats, business was good. Ruby Rae McDaniels, the attractive proprietress, served drinks and the best food in the territory. In her burgundy gown with black velvet ribbons crisscrossing the bodice, billowy sleeves and bustle, she moved among her customers with style and charm.

Luke Hanson gulped his second bourbon. When Ruby Rae headed toward him with the bottle, he waved his arm in refusal and politely tipped his hat. She moved over to where he stood at the end of the bar and asked, "What do you have planned for this afternoon?"

"Well," he replied, "the branding's all done and the cattle's grazing, so I thought I'd ride over to Slattery's Pond for a swim."

"That sounds heavenly," she sighed. "Will you be around this evening?"

"Most likely. There's not much else to do around here at night." He turned and slowly sauntered away as she placed her elbows on the bar and supported her chin in the palms of her hands. Watching the retreating figure, she noted the assurance of his step and the way his musculature shifted against the straining denim. As the swinging doors slowed to a standstill, she imagined herself embraced within his powerful arms. Her reverie was shattered, however, by the caustic voice of Trade Watkins.

"Hey, Ruby Rae! Quit daydreaming and fill up this here glass. Pronto!"

"Listen here, you. Be patient. You're not the only customer in my place. I may not be there when you want me, but I'm always right on time."

27

"What's a man gotta do to score points with a woman like you?"

She glanced at his greasy hair and the stubble on his face. "A bath and a shave might be a good place to start."

Luke Hanson untied the reins and patted the piebald stud that he'd raised from a foal. Swinging up into the saddle, he adjusted his boots in the stirrups. He removed his hat to wipe the sweat from his forehead with the back of his hand, and the harsh sun glinted off the gold ringlets that framed his tanned face. With his broad shoulders and straight back, he looked like he was born to ride high in the saddle.

He spurred his mount and rode west at a moderate pace until he reached the pond. Located at the foot of Rocky Point, the surrounding patches of scrub oak and larkspur gave it the appearance of an oasis.

After tying the reins around the trunk of a small tree, he stepped up onto a rock perched above the clear water. The first thing he noticed was that there was someone, already immersed, who had the same idea as himself. Sure enough, there was a horse nibbling the short grass across the pond, and a pile of clothing on a rock nearby. Luke stepped back and climbed to a higher position where he could observe unseen. He sat down and removed the small pouch containing tobacco and papers, and proceeded to roll himself a smoke.

The silence was broken by the splashing sounds of the swimmer who had finally surfaced for air. It was Richard Mannering, the temporary schoolmaster, who instructed the youngsters of Deep Gulch. As Luke inhaled deeply and watched the form moving athletically about, his mind drifted back to the day when Mannering had arrived at the small, wilderness town.

Up until a week prior to that day, Laura Mannering had been teaching at the one-room schoolhouse. She had travelled west from her native Boston to take up the position and had lived there happily until she had become unaccountably ill. Doc Preston advised her to stop working and get plenty of rest, so she summoned her brother, asking if he would help with the teaching chores while she recuperated. Her condition had finally improved and Richard, greatly relieved, decided to stay until recovery was complete.

When he stepped down from the stagecoach that day, Trade Watkins, the scoundrel of Deep Gulch, had confronted him in front of Ruby Rae's Saloon. "Stranger, who are ya and what do ya want?"

Looking a bit uncomfortable and out of place in his gray tweed four-button suit, starched collar and cravat, he offered his hand. "My name is Richard Mannering and I'm here to assist the school teacher, my sister. And whom, sir, do I have the pleasure of addressing?"

Trade ignored the outstretched hand. "Well, now don't you talk just like a reg'lar professor. So, you're the new schoolmarm, eh?"

The face of the young stranger became serious and he drew his frame up to its full height. "Sir, before you insult me any further, let it be known that I am well-practiced in the art of pugilism, and will give you a demonstration should your attitude persist." He crouched slightly and readied his fists.

Trade spat on the ground and taunted. "Pugilism? Is that some fancy style of French cooking?" He laughed and patted the piece of iron that hung threateningly at his hip. "This here gun does all my fightin'. You best stay clear. Y'hear?"

By that time a crowd had gathered in anticipation of a showdown, or at least a brawl. But Ruby Rae forced her way into the throng, took the stranger by the arm and led him to the teacher's cottage behind the schoolhouse at the end of the street. Luke had watched the scene and admired the way the young stranger had stood up to the town bully.

Luke ceased his reminiscence, stubbed out the tiny cigarette butt and jumped from the promontory to the ground. He made his way to the other side of the pond and stood on the rock by Richard Mannering's clothes. When the younger man emerged from the pond, he stood stark naked on the rock and stared into Luke Hansons' eyes.

"How's the water?" asked the overheated cowboy as his gaze took in the lithe, sculpted body that stood defiantly before him.

"Refreshing," said Richard.

Luke slowly unbuckled his holster and let it drop. He unbuttoned his plaid shirt, removed boots, trousers, skivvies and asked, "You feel like swimming some more? It looks like it could get mighty lonesome by yourself . . . wanna race?"

"Okay. To the far end and back?"

Luke nodded.

At the count of three, they dove into the cool water. Richard was back at the starting point waiting, with a look of mock superiority in his eyes, when Luke finally caught up. "Guess I'm out of practice," he chuckled.

"A little training would make you a great swimmer."

"Maybe someday you'll give me lessons?"

"I'd be glad to." Richard grinned. He splashed water at Luke's face and dunked his head, holding him under for a few seconds. When Luke's head bobbed up and his mouth gulped for air, Richard splashed him again and yelled, "Catch me if you can!"

He swam away while the other attempted pursuit. Looking back over his shoulder, he slowed his pace, allowing the cowboy to overtake him. Luke dove under, grabbed Richard by the ankles and pulled him down. They wrestled playfully in the middle of the pond until an overpowered Richard gave up. "Okay," he said between deep breaths, "you win."

As the two treaded water, Luke placed his hands on Richard's shoulders, then brushed his cheek with the backs of his fingers. Smiling, Richard touched the golden down on Luke's chest. He moved one hand lower to feel the tense muscles of Luke's washboard stomach, while the other hand gripped the firmness of his thigh. They embraced for a moment, then Luke said, "Let's go." They swam back, climbed out of the water and lay down on a blanket that Luke spread over the hot rock. When completely dry, they moved behind the formation and sat in the shade. Their eyes met. Luke took Richard's hand and held it. One thing led very smoothly to another and by the end of the afternoon, they had attained an intimacy that both had hoped for, but neither had ever thought possible.

☆ ☆ ☆

When Laura Mannering had become ill, Widow Turner volunteered to help out. She moved into the teacher's cottage, sleeping on the couch in the front room, to nurse the ailing Easterner. Doc Preston, not certain at first as to the nature of the illness, finally ascertained that it was simply exhaustion. Constant attention and lots of rest were what Laura required, and Widow Turner was an experienced prairie healer.

The afternoon session concluded and the children dismissed, Richard stopped by the cottage, a small A-frame trimmed in white, with shutters, a porch, and a garden in the backyard. Laura was sleeping and Richard gazed at her pale face and long auburn hair, noting that her breaths were long and easy. Quite a change from just a few days before. He leaned over and kissed her forehead, being extra careful not to awaken her.

Widow Turner poured a cup of tea for him and patiently answered all of his questions in the front room, the door to the bedroom slightly ajar. "She's sleeping less and eating more — a good sign. Yesterday she only ate some broth, but I got her to eat a soft-boiled egg this morning." She pulled a strand of gray hair from her forehead and smoothed the folds of her apron.

"And her sleep," asked Richard, "is it restful?"

"Most of the time. She's having fewer nightmares. She should be fine in no time at all."

Richard thanked her and patted her hand.

The sky was intermittently cloudy that day as Richard left the cottage and made his way down the plank walk. The street was deserted and the town locked in quietude as he approached the bank. Suddenly he heard someone scream for help and a gun shot rang out immediately thereafter. He was about to enter the bank when a man, clutching two large money bags, backed out the door. Richard grabbed him by the shoulder, spun him around and drove his fist into the robber's belly. The felon dropped the booty and fell to the ground, gasping for breath. Richard turned toward the door as another crook, with a six-gun in each hand, walked backwards out the door. Silently coming up behind the gunman, he seized his forearms from the rear and pressed his thumbs into the insides of the man's wrists. He dropped the guns and whirled around, only to have his jaw broken by Richard's swift uppercut. Rubbing his sore knuckles, Richard retrieved the money sacks and walked into the bank to return the loot and conduct his business.

Later that day, Luke strolled into Ruby Rae's, leaned against the bar and waited to be served.

"Hi there, handsome," called out Ruby Rae, her brown eyes sparkling, "the usual?"

"Yes'm."

Before she could get to him with the drink, Trade Watkins, who stood nearby, turned to Luke and smirked. "D'ja hear what happened?"

"No," said Luke, not particularly interested.

"You missed all the action. The schoolmarm beat up on two bank robbers," he chuckled.

"You want to step outside and repeat that?" asked Luke, a look of fury creeping onto his face. Trade realized something was wrong and went for his gun. But Luke, a lot quicker on the draw, shot it out of his hand. He placed his smoking revolver on the bar and said, "Outside."

They stood facing each other on the dusty street.

"You were saying something about —"

"Yeah," said Trade, "the schoolmarm —"

Luke grabbed Trade by his vest and hammered his fist into Trade's mid-section. He pushed him to the ground and fell on him, beating him with his tightly-clenched fists. Trade grabbed a handful of dirt and flung it at Luke's face. Tears obscured his vision and Trade's fist connected with his right eye. They rolled on the ground, kicking and punching, but Trade was no match for Luke and was quick to concede.

Luke slowly stood up, his fists still balled. With a stern voice he said, "The next time I hear you refer to Richard Mannering with anything less than respect, we can pick up where we left off. I'm warning you." He scooped up his hat, dusted it off and re-entered the saloon. After finishing his drink he returned his gun to its holster, tipped his hat to Ruby Rae and strode over to Richard's hotel room. He knocked and entered. "I hear you were a real hero today."

Richard gasped. 'What happened to you? You look like you got into a scrap with a polecat."

"Trade Watkins has a big mouth. I just shut it for him, that's all."

"That's the biggest shiner I've ever seen! Come and sit down over here."

Luke sat on the bed and Richard tended his wounds. He asked what happened and Luke told him. Shyly. Richard laughed. "Words can't hurt me . . . you shouldn't have gone to so much trouble."

"I couldn't help it. I, uh, think I love you."

☆ ☆ ☆

Jason T. Starrett, the bank president, gave Richard a reward — which he accepted reluctantly — and also insisted that Richard and a friend have dinner at Ruby Rae's, courtesy of the bank. Richard protested. "I just did what any honest person would have done."

"You must accept our acknowledgment of your noble deed. Just think, Mr. Mannering, it may cause others to become as conscientious as yourself." He clasped his hands and rested them on his rounded paunch.

Richard finally gave in, thanked the man, and invited Luke to dine with him on the following evening.

A large, noisy crowd was assembled in the smokey saloon. There were weary cowpokes, hungry travellers and fast women.

Some folks were eating and drinking, some gambling, while others were just listening to L. Washington Jones, the piano player. Recently arrived from St. Louis, the thin man with the gold tooth knew all the latest ragtime tunes.

When Ruby Rae placed the food before Luke and Richard —who sat adjacent to one another at a small, corner table— she eyed the cowboy and said, "I'm not doing anything later. Yourself?"

Luke looked away, embarrassed. "Aw shoot, Ruby Rae, you don't ever give up, do you?"

"Well, I just think a man like you could use a woman like me."

Luke blushed and struggled for something to say. Ruby Rae turned to Richard and said, "See if you can talk some sense into this fool."

"Madam," he almost choked, "I'll see what I can do."

When she turned to walk away, Richard winked at Luke. Luke deliberately dropped his spoon on the floor. The two men bent down to fetch it. When their faces came close together, their lips met for a brief, unobserved kiss. They sat upright and Luke tucked his napkin under his chin.

"How's Laura doing?"

"Growing stronger every day. I guess she was probably working too hard. That and the new territory must have been quite a strain. Widow Turner says she'll be up and around in no time."

Luke cut into his thick steak. "And what will you do when she's back at the schoolhouse?"

"Look around for work of some kind. I'm thinking of settling here for a while."

"To keep an eye on Laura?"

Richard casually sipped his wine and gestured toward Luke's swollen eye. "I was thinking about keeping an eye on you!"

Luke grinned. And winced. "Ouch," he said, and nodded at the bandage around Richard's knuckles. "You want me to cut up your steak?"

Richard laughed. Then smiled. They slowly ate the large meal—occasionally holding hands underneath the table— until they finished their coffee and were ready to depart.

Hammerthrower

Tom looks at the computer and waits for the screen to change. He senses Bentley staring at him, still angry because he was late. He'd had to stand in line at the post office. When he'd finally reached the window, the woman rummaged in the back for what seemed like an hour, only to return and hand him the package claim slip.

"It's probably been misfiled," she'd explained. He wanted to scream. *You stupid bitch! I'm late for work already . . . doesn't anything in this fucked-up city ever work?* But he'd smiled, given her his phone number so she could contact him when the package was found. "Thank you," he'd said and marched out the door. He muttered four-letter words and cursed the whole of civilization while racing to work. And finally ceased his ranting when he realized that people were looking at him the same way he looks at the ones who stand on street corners or sit in subway cars mouthing unintelligible nonsense. He quietly hummed an old song his grandfather used to sing while rapping on a banjo, "I'll Be Glad When You're Dead You Rascal, You."

"Code Entry" flashes on the screen and Tom wants to turn and look at Bentley as if to say, *See how fast I'm working, making up for lost time.* But Bentley is unaware of him, too busy cackling into the telephone, telling one of his friends about the utterly fabulous, too hot to mention—you won't believe it, darling—opening he'd been to the night before. When Tom had entered the business office, Bentley looked at his wristwatch, smiled lecherously and said, "If you had woken up with me, you wouldn't be late." Tom wished he had the nerve to reply, *If I'd woken up with you I'd have slit my wrists.*

34

Tom concentrates on the screen and begins to enter the new computer codes. He is halfway down the list when Bentley hangs up.

"Oh, Tom?"

"What."

"Did you see the memo about new code construction? We have to start using a new system so that the income earned from subscribers, general public and donations will be differentiated from each other, according to the run of the play, in quarterly segments."

"Oh?" He feels like smashing his fist through the computer screen but turns and fakes a smile. "There was nothing in my box about it," he pleads innocently. *Why didn't you tell me before I started, you dumb jerk.*

Bentley shuffles some papers on his desk and holds out the memo. "Here it is. I'm sure you'll be able to understand it without any explanation from me. I have a meeting with the Big Cheese in fifteen minutes, so let me tell you about the wonderful new play I saw last night. It's about a mother of six who's dying of cancer and she wins the New Jersey lottery and . . ."

Bentley's voice drones on and Tom seizes key words like 'comic,' 'intermission,' 'farce,' and 'direction,' but doesn't really listen, while thinking about how lonely he was when he woke up that morning. So lonely that he'd thought of Palmer Whittington for the first time in years. He began to evaluate his prospects and realized that the only person who has any sexual allure for him is the carpenter renovating the administrative offices above the off-Broadway theater. He'd started calling him Hammerthrower — too shy to try and find out his name — and as he thought of the hard, beefy body that always passed by his desk, his cock had woken up and reminded him that it had been a long time since he'd been naked with anyone. Brad, one of his best friends, is dying from AIDS and Tom is afraid for Brad and himself. The health crisis terrifies him. Moreover, he hasn't met anyone interesting for quite a while. And Hammerthrower, six feet, one hundred and eighty-five pounds of animal grace, passes by dozens of times every day and smiles. But so far nothing has been said. *He's probably straight anyway.*

". . . and at the end I didn't know if I should laugh or cry. It's that good. Best play of '85. Mark my words. I think I can get you a pair of comps. Interested?"

"A farce about cancer and lotteries? I'd rather watch a pineapple rot."

"Bitch! I try to be a nice guy . . ."

Asshole.

". . . and offer you two free tickets . . ."

Just so you can get me into bed, you miserable old queen.

". . . and you sit there making fun of a strong contender for the Pulitzer Prize . . ."

Shut up already, fatso.

". . . well, that's what I call gratitude."

"I'm sorry," says Tom, "just doesn't sound like my kind of play. And you know me, I'll say anything for a laugh."

"Well, I'm not laughing."

"I said 'I'm sorry'."

Tom turns to the computer terminal as Bentley walks out of the office, shaking his head. The phone on Bentley's desk begins to ring but Tom ignores it, preparing the new codes. He works it out so that each of the twelve possible financial entries can be immediately identified and retrieved with a series of six-digit numbers that indicate quarter, year and source. Satisfied that Bentley will find nothing to correct or complain about, he steps out of the office to fetch a cup of coffee. He spots Hammerthrower by the coffee machine and ducks into Claire's office.

"Good morning, Claire. How's Frick?"

"Impossible, as usual. How's Frack?"

"Obnoxious, as usual." They both grin.

"How about a cup of coffee," says Claire. "Rasputin and Scrooge should be in their meeting for at least a couple of hours."

"I'd love some. But you'll have to get it."

Claire removes her glasses and shakes out her hair. "Why me?"

" 'Cause Hammerthrower's hanging out by the coffee machine and if I tried to pour a cup with him so close I'd probably scald myself."

"Gimme a break!"

"I mean it. He really turns me on."

"He turns *all* of us on."

"Claire, do you know anything about him? Anything at all?"

"Nope. But if you want I can find out his name, address and social security number."

"Would you? Find out his name, I mean?"

"No problem. Coffee?"

"I'll answer your phone and take messages."

He sits at her desk, looking at her plants and ceramic knick-knacks. *Why can't I meet a guy who's as nice as Claire, romantic as Palmer and sexy as Hammerthrower?*

The phone rings and Tom grabs the receiver. "Hello?"

"Where's Claire? This is Mrs. Goldstein and I'm a subscriber and I just wanted to let you know that me and my husband —he's a doctor — really didn't like the last play and if you want us to subscribe again you're going to have to — "

"Excuse me, Mrs. Goldstein, would you hold please?" Click. "Hello?"

"Is Claire around?"

"She stepped out for a minute, can I take a message?"

"This is William."

The phone rings again. "Hold, please." Click. "Hello?"

"This is Robert down at the theater and our temperamental director just slugged out our temperamental leading man and they are consequently not talking, so I was wondering if Claire could come down and — "

"Hold, please."

Claire enters with two steaming styrofoam cups.

"Thank God you're back. I've got an angry subscriber on one, your boyfriend on two and a flustered production manager on three. How do you make it through a whole day of this?"

"Sex and drugs don't hurt."

"I leave you to your calls."

"How about lunch?"

"I'll stop by around 12:30."

"Becky," she says into the receiver, waving goodbye, "hold my calls for a while." Click. "Mrs. Goldstein? This is Claire. How are you today?"

Tom walks back to the business office with the coffee and begins to sort out the previous evening's box office receipts. A few minutes later he hears a knock at the door.

"Hi," says Hammerthrower, smiling.

"Oh, hi," says Tom. *Oh my God, I can't believe it, he spoke to me.* Tom clears his throat. "C C Can I help you?"

"Yeah. My name's George." He walks over and extends his hand.

"Tom." They shake.

"I've been doing some renovating around the office . . ."

As if I hadn't noticed.

". . . and there was a slight mistake on my paycheck . . ."

I'll fix it, I'll fix it!

". . . Look, see here? The decimal point is in the wrong place."

Tom looks at the check, then at George's bulging biceps, then back at the check.

"It's no problem. I can't change it, but Bentley can as soon as his meeting is over. Would you like to wait?"

"Thanks. Don't let me distract you."

"You can sit down right here," says Tom, indicating Bentley's chair. He turns to the terminal. *Oh, God, he's sitting right there. I wonder if he's looking at me? Okay, calm down, back to work. How can I work? I want to tear his clothes off and lick every inch of his body. Probably not even gay. But maybe.* Tom swivels his chair and faces George. "I've seen you around the office with your hammer and leveler and everything. How's it going?"

"Level."

"Huh?"

"It's called a level, not a leveler."

"Oh, I never knew that . . . so, how's it going?"

"Not bad. I should be done in about three weeks."

Three weeks. Gotta move fast. He tries to think of something clever to say. While stammering, waiting for inspiration, George suddenly speaks up.

"You know, Tom, I've been wanting to meet you."

"Me? Why?"

"Ever since I saw you dancing at the Manhole a few weeks ago I've wanted to meet you."

"You go to the Manhole?"

"Sometimes. When I feel like dancing."

Okay, so he goes to the Manhole. That doesn't mean he's gay.

"Since I broke up with my lover I've been getting out more."

He said lover, not girlfriend. Could this be true? "Oh, you just broke up," says Tom sympathetically. "I hope it wasn't too messy."

"Actually, I think he'll turn out to be a good friend."

I can't believe it. He's gay. What'll I say? Tell him how horny and lonely I've been? No. I'll ask him if he wants to see a movie with me next—

38

"I was wondering if you'd like to go dancing sometime?"

"You mean, with you?" Tom almost chokes.

"Of course."

"God, that would be great, how about—"

Bentley suddenly appears at the door. "My, my, party going on?" He looks at Tom, points to the computer and walks over to George. "Good day, Sir. I'm Bentley, the business manager. What can I possibly do for you?"

Tom turns to the computer and tries to ignore the conversation, with little success.

". . . so I just have to get my paycheck straightened out and everything will be fine."

"Hmm, let me see. Oh, this is easy. I'll make out a new one right away. Oh my dear, such arms! Which gym do you go to?"

"I don't go to a gym."

"I guess you naturally athletic guys don't have to."

"Actually, I'm not very athletic. Pretty handy, though."

"I'll bet you are. There you go."

"Thank you," says George.

"Perhaps we can get together sometime, lunch maybe? You can tell me all about how handy you are."

"Well, gee I don't know, Bentley? Bentley, well, that sounds nice, but I don't think my wife would understand. Bye."

Tom looks up and George winks at him as he exits. Bentley sits down and sighs, "Not a bad piece of meat, eh Tom? Too bad he's not on our team."

☆ ☆ ☆

Tom grasps the familiar doorknob with a trace of anxiety, not knowing what to expect. *Maybe a circus? No, it's a week night. A morgue, perhaps?* The door swings out, the red lights and loud music dancing out onto the sidewalk as he steps inside, glances around. The door closes behind him, imprisoning the sights and sounds within the bar's angular geometry. Not too crowded, but not dead either. There's a punk with studded ears and a tattoo of a scar on his cheek. *Thought they didn't allow those types west of Third Avenue.* Tom looks away before their eyes can connect.

Negotiating the bar. At the end near the door, pretty Derrick mixes a row of drinks with post-modernist choreography. *Too full of himself. Enough attitude to crash the sound barrier.* Tom makes his way to the far end of the bar and Arthur, *very nice, though he always seems so nervous,* hands him a light beer. He smiles and Tom smiles back, handing him a five. He waits for the change, leaves a twenty-five cent tip and walks to the jukebox.

Bruce Springsteen is moaning about "Dancing In the Dark" and Tom tries to imagine the rock star from New Jersey without clothing. *Nice.* Springsteen is replaced by Gloria Gaynor shouting, "I Am What I Am" as Tom moves to his favorite spot, near the cigarette machine. The speaker above thrusts slinky bass lines that keep his hips gyrating even when he's not crazy about the song itself.

He sips the beer and pictures Palmer Whittington right beside him. *Married to Elizabeth. Probably has two kids. Hires skinny hustlers and fucks them in motels in and around Baltimore and Washington. Waiting for Papa Whittington to die and leave him the undertaking business. Shit.*

Tom lights a cigarette and surveys the crowd. Plenty of flat stomachs and round butts but some are too young, too old or too hairy. Almost everyone has a moustache and beard. Tom likes the look but hates the feel of bristly hair scratching his face. He recalls the time his lips were scraped until they felt like sandpaper.

He notices a cute guy with a hard, compact body leaning against the bar. His moustache looks soft, like corn-husk fibers. *Not bad. I'll just stand here, try to look like I'm not too interested, but willing. When he glances this way I'll smile. He'll smile back. I'll wait a second to see if he makes a move. If not, I'll just walk right over and shake his hand. The name's Tom. Pleased to meet you. I'll tell him about the theater and look into his eyes, accidentally on purpose brush his hip with my hand. He'll kiss me and suggest that we go to his apartment —*

A man with build, facial hair and coloring, all similar to Tom's intended, enters his field of vision and joins the man whom Tom is mentally seducing. They kiss, exchange a few words and are out the door, while Tom silently curses, wondering if they're friends or lovers. *Probably lovers,* he decides, grateful that he hadn't yet made the move that would have resulted in rejection and embarrassment.

The throbbing bass line that buoys the Supremes leaps out of the speakers and Tom's body is enslaved by the rhythm. "You Can't Hurry Love" he sings along in a silent falsetto, his free hand adding punctuation to the lyric. He throws the cigarette butt to the floor and stomps it out as two slim Hispanic guys enter the bar, whispering in each others' ear, tittering over some private joke.

He remembers being fifteen. Mr. and Mrs. Whittington were away for the weekend. Palmer invited Tom to spend the night. Tom told his parents the invitation had come from Mrs. Whittington. They danced together for the first time in Palmer's rich-kid bedroom. The soundtrack provided by the Supremes. Then they slept together. Waking up at short intervals all night long, tentatively touching each others' body. *Gotta stop thinking about Palmer, concentrate on Hammerthrower, I mean George. Maybe tomorrow I'll just walk over to him and—*

"How ya doin'? Sam's the name. What's yours?" Tom turns his head to the left, the direction the voice comes from. A short, balding man with a jelly-belly smiles and offers his hand. Tom refuses it and looks away. He almost delivers his lecture on cruising etiquette. *It's not fair to approach a stranger in a bar who has not had the opportunity to indicate whether he is interested. Attacks from the rear are an intrusion. Definitely not in good taste.*

"Fuck you," says Sam, wandering away like someone had just kicked his teeth in. Tom wonders what Sam's response would have been like if he'd delivered the lecture. He envisions him sobbing and is glad he's kept quiet.

He sips the beer and looks around. Not much to choose from. Derrick leans against the bar, as though posing for a Calvin Klein ad while Arthur, *nice, average-looking Arthur* pops beer cans and mixes cocktails. An older man—overweight, wearing a tacky toupee—hovers near the jukebox and Tom thinks that the sight of this man naked would probably make him throw up.

The Mutant Slime jump out of the speakers extolling the pleasures of "The Road To Hell" amid the chainsaw buzz of decibel-crazed electric guitars. *This ought to wake everyone up.*

The door opens and Carlton, an ex-trick enters. *Oh no!* Tom hopes that Carlton will not notice him. He remembers going to Carlton's apartment one night, expecting the usual kissin' and huggin', suckin' and fuckin', only to discover that Carlton's primary pursuit is having his face straddled. Tom, not wanting to appear rude, sat on Carlton's face, embarrassed, wishing he had not accepted the invitation to spend the night. When Carlton said, "Okay, let 'er go," Tom had no idea what he meant. "Bombs away!" urged Carlton and Tom, suddenly enlightened, got up, dressed faster than he ever had before and

41

left in silence. If Carlton approaches, Tom will say I *don't shit on command*, a phrase he has prepared for such an occasion.

Carlton wanders past and Tom recalls the one time he was able to think of a clever, spontaneous rejoinder. Always terrific with snappy quips long after they could be useful, Tom fears that he is doomed to always thinking, *If I'd only said . . .* But the muse had come to his rescue when his parents had found some physique magazines beneath his bed when he was sixteen. Confronting their son, Tom's father looked blank as his mother queried, "Are you a homo?" With matchless timing Tom answered, "All day, every day and all through the night." Shaken at first by his confession, his parents were reassured by the confidence with which he'd replied. As though he could take care of himself and handle any situation. The subject was never brought up again, however, his parents did not reenter his room until he'd moved away, and they acted like they'd never found out.

Tom leaves the beer can on the ledge that runs around the periphery of the room and Arthur has one ready for him when he reaches the bar. "Thanks," he says, handing the money to Arthur.

"On the house," says Arthur who taps the bar, smiles, and turns to refill the ice tray.

Willie Nelson sings "All Of Me" and Tom hums along even though Ol' Willie records too frequently and suffers from overexposure. Too bad. A handsome black man with a sexy bubble-butt and muscular thighs walks toward the jukebox, and though Tom likes his body and smooth skin, the beads and cowrie shells braided to the man's scalp cause his interest to subside. He's back at his usual spot and directly behind him, two men are talking a little too loudly.

"This is the third time in less than four months that someone I know's been diagnosed with AIDS. It's scary."

"I read something about a strain of virus recently detected in sheep and it said — "

"Sheep? Are you kidding? First it was pigs, now it's sheep . . . I don't want to talk about it."

And I don't want to hear about it. Tom remembers all of the good times he's had with Brad, Steve and Patrick — dinners, discos and drugs before separating to search for sex — and now Brad is lying in a hospital bed, just waiting to die. *Life sucks!*

Willie Nelson is nudged off the turntable by Patti Smith and Tom goes to the john. He places his beer on the sink and pees, then takes a joint from his cigarette pack. Three large tokes are drawn and exhaled, the joint stubbed out and reunited with the cigarettes. He returns to his usual spot. "Girls Just Want To Have Fun" he sings and sways, the grass relaxing him completely. He peers at the crowd through new eyes and sees a handsome, thirtyish guy at the bar. He smiles. The guy smiles back. Tom is by his side.

"Hi. Tom."

"Jean-Hugh."

"Huh?"

"Jean-Hugh," he says very slowly. They shake hands. "You come here often?"

"No, just visiting."

Shit! "Where are you from?"

"Montreal."

"That's nice." Tom looks at Jean-Hugh and thinks about all of the tourists he's entertained since moving to New York. And how each one took a tiny piece of his soul away. *There's Guy in Chicago, Michael in Shreveport, Justin in Albuquerque, even Bruno in Zurich. But what good are they so far away?* He decided to get involved sexually only when there is the possibility for some kind of relationship other than a penpal.

"What do you do?" asks Jean-Hugh.

"I'm an accountant. It's pretty boring." Tom takes advantage of the silence between songs. "Think I'll go and play the jukebox. Nice meeting you." Tom slowly walks to the jukebox, pretends he's inserting some quarters and presses a few random numbers.

The Judds pop out of the speakers and ask, "Why Not Me?" their passionate yearning impossible to ignore. *Goddamn. Another lonely night.* He finishes the beer and walks to the door. *Do I want to go to Video Village and watch the pretty boys swoon over Alexis and Krystle, or do I want to go to sleep?* It takes two seconds to choose his bed over the video screen. He waves to Arthur, leaves the barroom, and embraces the cool night air that's been waiting for him behind the familiar door.

☆ ☆ ☆

Tom chuckles to himself as he mentally composes a list of the absurd titles that have been produced at the No Exit Theater: *Moon Pie Gunner, Granny's Beer-Stained Shawl, Play Dead, Racing To Sleep, Things That Go Hump In The Dark.*

43

As auditing time approaches, it's Tom's task to inventory all financial records for the three previous years. Every ledger must balance perfectly, every dime be accounted for, or the theater will lose it's nonprofit status. Each afternoon, Tom checks and double-checks the paperwork of a closed production. As Bentley has planned it, he will be right on schedule for the auditing team that will appear in two weeks. Bentley sits at his desk reading the reviews of the play about motherhood, cancer and the New Jersey lottery. Tom scans figures on the computer screen. The telephone rings and Bentley answers it. "It's for you." He puts the call on hold and hangs up as Tom lifts his receiver.

"Hello." Tom knows Bentley is listening, trying to figure out what's being said on the other end. "Hi, Steve, how are you." Bentley pretends he's still reading. "Fine. Everything's okay. What's up?" Bentley's ear strains to catch any sound that might escape the receiver. "No! It can't be." Panic spreads across Tom's face as he turns away from Bentley. "What time? Was he alone?" Bentley looks at Tom with sympathy. "What do you mean, 'private'?" A tear falls from Tom's eye. "When's the memorial service?" He reaches into his pocket for a handkerchief. "Thanks, Steve. I'll call you tonight."

Tom blows his nose. Bentley puts the paper down. "Your friend, the one with AIDS, what's his name?"

"Brad."

"Is it over?"

"Yeah, he died this morning. Christ, thirty-two years old."

"When's the funeral?"

"His family doesn't want any of his queer friends at the funeral. We're going to have our own memorial service next week sometime."

"Can I get you anything?"

"No. Thanks."

"Would you like to take the afternoon off?"

"No, I'm all right. Can't say I wasn't expecting it." Tom decides to change the subject. *Mustn't get too chummy with Bentley, he'd get the wrong idea.* "Besides, who'll go over the accounting for *Crapshit*, I mean *Slapschtick*?"

"Why do you always make fun of our plays? And why do you always tune me out? I want us to be friends."

We can't be friends because I can't stand the sight of you or the sound of your whiny voice. "I never mix work and friendship."

44

"You can come up with a better line than that."

None that I dare say out loud. He punches the keyboard, the green neon digits popping up on the small screen.

"I have a board meeting at three, Tom, and I have to have a quick conference with the Big Cheese beforehand, so I'm leaving now. Take messages and I'll return calls tomorrow morning."

"Okay."

He feeds the computer with one half of his brain and thinks about his career trajectory with the other. He'd started at the theater as a temporary receptionist, and was hired on a permanent, fulltime basis after several months. One year after that he'd been shifted to assistant to the Production Manager and eventually snagged the coveted post of assistant to the Business Manager. As soon as Bentley is promoted to assistant General Manager, Tom will be in charge of the business office. It's an easy job that pays well, and Tom can select his assistant from the pool of underlings waiting for a shot at promotion. After that he'll only have to find his perfect soul mate and life will be everything he could hope for.

He finishes checking the final numbers and returns the data to the memory banks. Lifting the telephone receiver, he dials for an outside line.

"Good afternoon. May I speak with Patrick, please. This is Tom calling."

"Hold, please."

He drums his fingers on the desk and hums a ditty from his childhood.

"Tom? Patrick here. Have you heard about Brad?"

"Yeah. Steve called a little while ago."

"I just spoke to him."

"How do you feel?" asks Tom timidly.

"Like shit. You?"

"Worse than shit . . . you want to meet at the bar after work, try to drown it a bit?"

"That'd be good."

"See ya there." He buzzes reception and gets Becky on the line. "I'm stepping out of the office for a while and Bentley's at a meeting. Could you hold the calls, please?" He walks into Claire's office and sits down, waiting until she's off the telephone.

"Always a pleasure talking to you, Mrs. Goldstein," she wrinkles her face in disgust, " 'bye now."

"Hi."

"I'm tired of that old bitch," sighs Claire.

"I'm tired of *that* old bitch," says Tom, hiking his thumb toward the business office.

"So, what's new? Quick, before the phone rings."

"You want the good or the bad first?"

"Hmmm, the good."

"I met Hammerthrower yesterday. His name's George and he's on my team."

Claire shakes her head. "That's a relief. I thought there was something wrong with my hair! And what's the bad news?"

"My friend, Brad, the one I told you about—"

"The one with AIDS?"

"Yeah."

Claire places her hands on Tom's knees. "I'm so sorry, for him, for you. All you guys. I know it must be rough."

"Thanks for letting me get it off my chest. It really helps."

"Tom? You wanna meet me on the roof later? We'll smoke a joint, talk a bit. Might help."

"What time?"

"Three-thirty. The board meeting should just be getting underway."

"Sounds great."

"Be there or be square," she intones.

"Later."

Tom steps out into the hall, walks to the men's room and enters. He's alone. He washes his face with cold water, and is drying his hands on a paper towelette as the door swings open.

"Tom, how are you?"

"George!" They shake hands, study each others' face and both begin talking at the same time.

"Go ahead," says George.

"I just wanted to apologize for Bentley, interrupting us that way yesterday."

"Is he like that all the time?"

"You mean pompous and overbearing? Yeah, it's what he does best."

"Doesn't he get on your nerves?"

"Yup, he drives me crazy. But I think he'll be promoted soon and then everything'll be okay."

George smiles. "I think we were talking about going dancing sometime."

Tom blushes. "I'd really like that."

"You free tonight?"

Tom almost spills the news about Brad, but quickly reconsiders. *There's plenty of time to compare AIDS notes.* "I can't make it tonight. But anytime after."

"How about tomorrow night?"

Tom wants to embrace George, lick his ear and press their bodies together. A slight shudder tiptoes up his spine. "Tomorrow night is perfect."

George hands Tom a business card. "My phone number. Call me after work tomorrow and we'll arrange something. You want to go to the Manhole?"

"That would be fun."

They both wait for the other to make a move or say something, but they remain still and silent. Tom leans forward as George wraps his arms around his waist and draws him closer. Breathless, they squeeze each other and bring their lips together, jumping apart as the door swings open. They both nod at the intruder, an auditioning actor, no doubt.

"Well," says Tom.

"Well," says George, "I'll stop by the office later and pick up that W-2 form."

"Right-O," says Tom, "see you later." He walks back to the office, touching the pocket that contains the card with George's number. *I hope there's a kind soul with smelling salts around when I realize what just happened and faint.* He throws back his head and laughs out loud. Entering the business office, he hums a happy tune that's been dancing in his memory for as long as he can remember.

Love's Jealous Fury

"This corset is *killing* me! There's a stay poking my right armpit . . . and it hurts!" Alex walked to the mirror in the small, box-like room that reeked of unlaundered sweat socks. The mustard-yellow carpet and mayonnaise-white walls seemed to match the stale odor. Vincent sighed and struggled with the zipper, finally yanking it, in fits, to the neckline. "Can I breathe now?" gasped Alex.

"Don't you dare. There'll be sequins and bugle beads embedded in the walls, floor and ceiling."

Alex eyed himself in the three-way mirror and frowned. "Magenta is definitely not my color." He turned to the left and looked over his shoulder. "And this wig! It's all wrong. I should've brought the Veronica Lake."

Vincent removed the cigarette from his lips and stubbed it out. Grabbing the hairbrush which lay alongside the ashtray, he advanced toward the mirror. "Perhaps if I tease it up a bit here and there. You know, you really don't look too bad. I've known *real* girls who would kill for your waist," he said, sucking in the stomach that bulged slightly over his jeans. "There! Is that any better?"

Alex turned to the right and scrutinized his image. "Hmmm, that's not too bad . . . maybe a bit more rouge. What do you think?"

"I think you're nuts, but don't let that stop you. Did I tell you this was crazy? Did I?"

Alex waddled to the vanity table. "This girdle is too tight."

"You don't even have the heels on yet and you're moving like a Mack truck."

Alex sat down very slowly and groaned.

48

Vincent grimaced. "Successful women authors, when they are sitting down, do not open up like the gates to Buckingham Palace. Put those legs together!"

Someone pounded on the thin door. "Five minutes!"

"Thank you," said Alex. Vincent pinched his arm. "Er, thank you," he purred, stretching his voice two octaves higher.

"You've got to be more careful," whispered Vincent.

"I know, I know." Alex stared wistfully into the light bulb-encrusted vanity mirror. "And I still have to get these gargantuan feet into those tiny shoes. Would you give me a hand?"

"Of course. That's why God created literary agents."

☆ ☆ ☆

The three-piece band attempted a Vegas fanfare beneath the burning kleig lights and Don James, wearing a blue serge suit with a plum-colored ascot, beamed a smile into Camera One. The studio audience roared on cue.

"And now, ladies and gentlemen, my next guest is the lovely and tantalizing author of the book that *everyone* is talking about. The woman who created *Love's Jealous Fury*, Antonia Harlequinette!"

The applause sign lit up and the crowd clapped wildly as she sashayed to the empty chair by the host's desk.

"Antonia, you, of course, know Biff LeGrande."

"Why yes, we met backstage."

The football star/deodorant salesman stood up and pumped her gloved hand. "A pleasure."

"Oh Biff, the pleasure's all mine!" She waited for Don and Biff to sit and finally realized they were waiting for her. Lowering herself into the plush chair, she smoothed the folds of her gown, tearing off a few hundred beads. They scattered on the floor and everyone pretended not to notice.

"So, Antonia, are you enjoying the success of your new book?"

"Well, Don, I'd be lying if I denied it."

"It's been a bestseller for months. Were you surprised?"

"One can never predict what people want to read. One simply writes and hopes for the best. Have you read it?"

"Well, uh, not yet, but it's right at the top of my list."

"That's such a comfort," she said, toying with the cameo that dangled in the hollow of her throat.

"Tell me, Antonia, what inspired you to write this story?"

"I'll tell you, Don, I just observe what's going on around me and turn it into literature."

"Are you saying that your book is autobiographical?"

"Not exactly. Helen Handwerker, that's the heroine, she has some of my character traits, but mostly it's from my imagination. I mean, I would never shoot a man in bed. I'd at least wait until he got dressed." She waited for the yucks but the laugh sign did not flicker. The color slowly returned to the cheeks of Don James. He mumbled something that was inaudible and, retaining his composure said, "We'll be right back after this brief message."

All eyes focused on the monitors. Sandwiched in between the one about starving children and the one about dog food was a commercial for Secure. Biff LeGrande, grimy and sweating, sits down on the locker room bench and sighs. Then, he's taking a shower, the camera ogling his ample chest and arms. Now, he's standing in front of his locker, a white towel wrapped around his waist, holding a red and blue cylinder. "Be safe with Secure. Confidence in a can." Suddenly fourteen jiggly blondes surround him, pawing and shrieking. He appears to be enjoying the attention.

The bandleader signalled the familiar eight bars, and the applause sign flashed its message with urgency.

"Welcome back, ladies and gentlemen. I'm sitting here with Biff LeGrande, who just gave one of his characteristically scintillating locker room performances, and Antonia Harlequinette, the author of *Love's Jealous Fury*. Tell me, Antonia, are you married?"

"No."

"Have you ever been?"

"Well, yes, I mean no, not in the legal sense."

"You've *lived* with men?"

"That's right. And women."

Don James shook his hand as if he'd placed it on a hot waffle iron. "Not at the same time, I hope!" He chuckled at his own joke and the laughter and applause signs roused the audience to hysteria.

"Gosh," said Biff, "that sounds pretty racy to me!"

Antonia cast him an icy glance.

"But sexy too!" he added.

"So, Antonia," said the host, "are we to assume that you don't approve of marriage?"

She tossed her hair over her shoulder and moistened her lips. "Not for myself. A great writer must have many love affairs. Marriage only gets in the way." She waited for a response but the laughter sign lay dormant and the audience remained silent.

"Well," said Don, "Antoniait'sbeengreattalkingtoyouhurry backandseeusagainsometimeokay? Nowafterabriefmessagewe'll bebackwithournextguest."

☆ ☆ ☆

"You were sensational!" A happy Vincent hugged a sheepish Alex.

"You don't think I blew it?"

"Blew it? You were on television! It'll sell books! This is America!"

Alex pulled the wig from his head and reached around to unzip his gown. "It's a good thing they don't have a sign that says *attack*." He removed the shoes. "Do you really think I was convincing as . . . a woman? I mean — "

A fist pounded the dressing room door.

"Uh, who's there?" chimed Antonia.

"It's Biff. Biff LeGrande."

"Just a moment, please." Hastily replacing the wig, she strode to the door and flung it open like Loretta Young on methedrine. "Come in, come in. This is my agent, Vincent Spinetti. Vince, meet Biff LeGrande."

The two men shook hands as Antonia closed the door. Biff glanced around the room, then fixed his eyes on Antonia. "You may have fooled the bimbos out in televisionland, but you didn't fool me for one second."

Antonia stiffened. "Why, Biff, whatever do you mean?"

"Come off it, sweetie." He pulled the wig from Antonia's head and, pushing his hair from his forehead, put it on. Swaggering toward the mirror, he placed his hand on his hip and studied his reflection. "This is definitely more me than you."

Antonia gasped. Vincent looked stunned.

"Just between us," said Biff, studying the makeup on the table, "I won the Miss Drag San Francisco contest in 1982."

Vincent suppressed a giggle. "You?"

"Moi," he said, "and I could probably win it this year too, if I had the time. I have a collection of wigs and gowns that makes Antonia's — "

"Alex."

"Alex's wardrobe look like rags."

"I never would have guessed," said Vincent.

"Me neither," said Alex.

"When I retire from football I'm planning on opening a chain of drag boutiques: LeGrande Dames—feminine attire for the discriminating man."

Alex and Vincent looked at one another in astonishment.

"Well, I've got to go now," said Biff.

"See you on the Carson show," said Alex.

"You bet." He departed, slamming the door.

Alex whispered, " He's very cute."

"He's not your type," said Vincent, "he's mine."

Alex moaned. "If I don't get out of this corset soon I'll kill myself. I feel like I'm in a Chinese finger trap."

"It's a good thing we brought the muumuu. Here."

Alex undressed and slipped into the comfy folds of pink and green cotton. "So, it's back to the hotel."

"Right." Vincent lit a cigarette.

"And tomorrow?"

"Baltimore. It'll be a snap. You're to be the Guest of Honor at a fund-raising luncheon for the Elks."

"Are you *serious?*" Alex sat down and put on his bunny slippers.

"No. Actually, you're going to address a group from Women Against Pornography."

"VINCENT!"

"Okay, okay, just kidding. It's a symposium on violence at a Romance Writer's Workshop."

"I think I can handle that."

"One thing, Alex?"

"Yes?"

"A bit less mascara, perhaps, and uh, no more bugle beads. Okay?"

The Bold Sailor

Time itself cannot touch you. It is the measurement, the containment, the stretching and contracting of the moments that leaves scars. My friends say that I will forget. Or that he will come back. As if the two were dependent. But something tells me he will never come back. And I know that I will never forget him. I can count on this — on myself. Not that I am so remarkably reliable. It just seems that everything else is much less so.

I had noticed him sitting across from me on the subway. He smiled and I imagined a terrific body beneath the loose-fitting designer jeans, but I looked away. I never smile on the subway or in bars. The consequences could be dangerous. That night he walked over to me at the bar. Was it a coincidence that I'd seen him earlier, or had he been following me around? I'm still not certain. Blond and balding slightly, his hard body packed into old Levi's, he had a tattoo on his right bicep: USN.

"What d'ya call that there you're drinkin'?" he asked.

"I don't call it anything, it's . . ."

"Vodka and cranberry juice."

"That's correct," I said. I was surprised but tried not to show it.

"I been watchin' them makin' your drinks for a few nights now. I wanted to buy you one but didn't know what to call it."

"Vodka and cranberry juice."

"Right." He looked at me nervously, expecting me to say something, so I did.

"What's USN?"

"Huh?"

I touched his arm. "The tattoo."

53

"United States Navy."

"You used to be a sailor?"

"Still am. But I'm gettin' out soon. You?"

"I'm a painter."

"Pictures or houses?"

"Paintings. And I work at the library."

"The liberry?"

"No, the library."

I didn't make it easy for him; I never make it easy for anyone. A man's got to be careful. But I liked him and invited him to my loft. We spent the night together. I didn't find out his name until the following morning.

☆ ☆ ☆

I'm always thinking about the time I spent with him. It's involuntary. I try to hold onto the good memories and not feel the pain. Difficult. Would I rather not have the memories at all? No, these are all I have to treasure, though the reminder of my present loneliness is the price. The sailor comes and goes, leaving behind a trace of salty sea air. I sniff and it stings my nostrils.

I know the songs of sailors. From before the steam engine. When ships sailed into the unknown on muscle-power and sweat. Men sang songs to make the work go easier. And the songs of home that lulled them to sleep at night. To dream about the loved ones. Some were content living among all that man-power. Others dreamed that the Captain's pretty cabin boy was a girl in disguise.

There among the barflies, so many hairdressers in cowboy drag, was what I'd been searching for. A man who loved men. I presumed he possessed all of the fine attributes of manhood: honesty, courage, ambition. Neither an intellectual or a disco queen. He'd never seen a Broadway show or been to the opera. I was amazed.

The morning after our first night together he nudged me with his knees and asked if I was awake. I turned and looked at his cheery face. I offered to make some coffee and he finally introduced himself. "By the way, m'nam   Wayne. Wayne Bedford."

We shook hands. The first time I'd ever done that in bed. He hugged me. We kissed. He started to tickle me but it was far too early for laughter. I jumped out of bed and heated some water.

We got together again that night and the next morning I persuaded him to remove his belongings from the YMCA and spend the rest of his leave with me. There was so much that I wanted to discover about sailors and I figured he might learn a few things from me as well.

☆ ☆ ☆

I know the songs of the sea. From before scientists started taping the sounds of whales and dolphins to be vivisected by musicologists. I have the records that Wayne bought for me. *Whaling and Sailing Songs From The Days of Moby Dick, Blood Red Roses.* And I found one at the library called *We'll Go To Sea No More.* Tough songs about hard work, squalid lives and treacherous companions. Gentle songs about love and separation.

Perhaps he joined the Navy because of some romantic dream about the old times. He knew that the days of piracy and adventure were over. But he'd been raised in a coastal fishing town in New England, originally settled by Portuguese immigrants. The tales and songs had been passed down from father to son for generations. But being out on the sea in the Twentieth Century was something different. The latest news, political and cultural, is not foreign to the modern sailor unless he chooses isolation in order to escape contemporary life. I was never certain about Wayne's motives. Every time I asked him to tell me about the Navy all he ever said was, "Drank a lot. More than you'd believe. Smoked a lot of hash. Had guys in every port. You can have an Eyetalian or an A-rab for a song." Then he'd wink and laugh. A deep, throaty chortle that would redden his cheeks and make his eyes shimmer. "But nothing like you," he would add and wrap his arms around me, kissing and squeezing, summoning something from within that would smolder and ignite until the two of us fell asleep, tangled together on damp, rumpled sheets.

☆ ☆ ☆

I don't sell many paintings. That is, as many as I should. But I sell more than I did before I met Wayne. He taught me to be more aggressive. And that pleasing people is not sinful.

I remember the first time I showed him my work. My loft has stacks of canvasses everywhere, but I don't think he so much as glanced at one until I asked for his opinion. I selected four recent efforts and leaned them against the empty wall which serves that particular purpose. He lit a cigarette and carefully studied each one. "I don't know what they mean, but I like the colors."

"They don't *mean* anything."

"Then why paint 'em?"

"To create something that is appealing to the eye."

"I like paintin's of flowers and bowls of fruit. Oceans and hillsides. Y'know, stuff that's real."

"Well, my work is . . ."

"Work? You call this *work*?" He snuffed out the cigarette and asked if I wanted to go for a drink. I declined and spent the evening reading. He returned a few hours later and made love to me as though atoning for some horrible crime.

The next night he insisted on taking me to dinner. He wanted to go to a semi-fashionable restaurant where the employees and clientele were gay males, and a LaCoste shirt and clean jeans were considered dressy enough. He said and did everything with great formality. I grasped that this was a big event for him and did not correct him when he mispronounced the wine he'd selected. I assumed his pose and acted as though we were at the Captain's table.

Over coffee he told me that he'd decided to terminate his naval career and look for a civilian job. "Could I stay with you and share the rent?" He reached for my hand, gallantly kissed it and smiled. I felt like the one who catches the bouquet at the end of the wedding. He looked like he'd just won the lottery.

☆ ☆ ☆

He called last night, the first time in about three months, but he was too drunk to really communicate. I kept asking where he was calling from but never got a coherent answer.

I couldn't sleep. I pictured him stripped to his jockey shorts and recalled the sensation of his skin against my own. I changed positions, stomach down, and tried to think about something else but the images would fly at me, taunting like a horde of angry demons.

I called the library the next morning and told the branch manager that I had the flu. Lots of fluids and plenty of rest, he suggested. I couldn't face the strangers who passed in and out of the book-lined fortress that I fantasized as my own. The people who came in to read or escape the weather never bothered me. And the erudite souls who truly love books, reserve several at once and return them on time are so few. It's the others who occasionally rouse the monster in me. They break spines, fold corners and confuse John Ashbery with John Berryman. I despise them, and by extension, the job. Sometimes, when the library is completely empty and it's just me and all those words, I feel a contentment that I've never found anywhere else. The silence is a symphony of white noise and when I close my eyes I can hear the voices arising from the pages discussing love and death, arguing theories, trading juicy gossip.

My real work is altogether different. I try to capture shapes, colors and textures with oil and canvas. Then I must persuade some suburban harridan to buy the work by convincing her that after I die, which could be anytime considering the squalor of my existence, she shall have made a smart investment. Business is a pursuit that has never interested me, nor have I been successful in mastering its protocol. I suppose I could have found work that pays better than the library. But I probably would not have found the time to paint, and if magically found, not known what to do with it. Wayne said he wanted lots of money. In fact, he informed me, he was one of the few who would know what to do with a fortune, should he ever be in possession of one.

☆ ☆ ☆

The money and hashish that he had accumulated for his leave were beginning to disappear; he'd spent two hundred dollars on a three-piece suit. Burnt sienna. I came home from work one day and found him sitting on the bed, his suit disheveled and sweat-soaked. He clutched the classified ad section of the *Times* with several positions circled in pencil. Leaning back, he tossed the paper aside and clasped his hands behind his head. "Well, I registered with an employment agency and they made me up a resume. Resume?" I nodded. "And I'm supposed to call tomorrow."

"How does it feel, job-hunting in the big city?"

"It's fun! Lots of good-lookin' guys everywhere. I got lost, though. Finally just got in a taxi and gave the guy your, I mean our address."

☆ ☆ ☆

Ever since Wayne left I have kept myself so busy that time is something that is no longer part of my conscious thought. I cannot gauge or measure it and have lost the ability to control it. I seem to exist apart from — above or below, I'm not certain which — the rush of time. Haven't escaped it. I can feel myself aging. Slowly. But still, somehow, I am removed.

On the third day of Wayne's search for employment I returned home and found him cursing the heat and concrete sidewalks.

"What's the matter?"

"I called my sister to wire me some money 'cause it looks like I might not find a job as fast as I thought. Anyway, she told me that Mom is in the hospital."

"Is it serious?"

"Brain tumor."

"Oh, my God!" I hugged him and comforted him as best as I could.

"I'm gonna catch the 9:47 bus."

"Is there anything I can do? Do you feel like eating something?" He nodded. I glanced at the clock. "Just enough time to get some groceries. After we eat I'll help you pack and we'll go to the station together. All right?"

When I returned from the supermarket, however, he was gone. He'd packed his belongings and left the keys in the mailbox. I could not find a note with a telephone number where he could be reached.

The next day I received a call from the employment agency. Wayne had been accepted for the position of clerk at a "chic private hotel." I said I'd have him call as soon as I heard from him.

I went about my work, absent-mindedly, for several weeks, wondering what was going on. Eventually I received my phone bill which registered a long distance call to somewhere in Massachusetts, "between Boston and the Cape," as Wayne had once said. I walked around for a few days with the bill in my pocket, anxious to call, afraid of what I'd find out.

Late at night, a few days later, I dialed. His sister answered. He wasn't there nor did she know where he was stationed. I introduced myself and she said that Wayne had spoken of me. "As long as I have you on the phone," I said, dying of curiosity but fearful that I was intruding, "I'd just like to find out how your mother is doing."

"What do you mean? She's fine, as far as I know."

"I see. That's a relief."

"Did Wayne tell you she was sick or something?"

"In a word, yes."

"Oh, honey, that's just Wayne's way. He's been making up stuff like that ever since he was a kid."

A few days later I received a hastily scribbled note from Wayne in which he apologized for having lied about his mother's health. He went on to explain that he was afraid he'd never find a job and would not allow himself to be supported by another.

I didn't really speak to anyone for weeks. When friends would call I'd say that I was busy and would get back to them when I was able.

I'm desperate to let him know that he'd been accepted for a job, but he usually calls when drunk and never lets me know where he is so that I can write to him. Although he stays in touch, communication is difficult.

All I have now is work, time and memories which function together like an automated Mobius strip. And I still have the records he gave me. There's one song in particular that constantly runs through my mind. It's about a bold sailor who leaves his lover to go to sea, each one keeping half of a broken coin. Years later when they meet, they do not recognize each other at first, but the parts of the coin match perfectly and they realize that they have been reunited. Sometimes I have a dream that is like a surreal film of that song with Wayne and myself as the main characters, mandolins and concertinas snaking across the soundtrack. Only when we meet again we recognize each other instantly. The two halves of the coin, however, do not fit.

ALL ABOUT EVE

1. The Clothes Make The Man
2. The Morning After The Night Before

The Clothes Make the Man

Robbie and I were already in our pajamas and bathrobes when the first guests began to arrive. Mr. Williams appeared at the door as a football player, and his wife had on a bonnet, chewed a teething ring and had a plastic training potty strapped around the enormous diaper that clung to her waist. I took their coats as Robbie, fifteen months younger than me, led them into the living room.

"Who was that?" asked Father as I passed by my parents' bedroom.

"Pete and Rona," I said and deposited their outerwear on the bed in the guestroom.

"C'mere and help me," he called just as I was about to re-join Robbie, sneaking cigarettes and canapes. As I helped Father fasten the large suspenders of his clown costume, he chuckled to himself in the full-length mirror and said, "The clothes make the man!" That was his philosophy of life, and it had been drilled into Robbie and I every time we went shopping for clothes or dressed to go out. This was the first time he had ever said it in jest, though, and I was greatly relieved to discover that he was capable of joking about it.

The doorbell rang again, and after dealing with the coats, Robbie and I stole upstairs to our bedroom, where we had hidden the forbidden booty. We were ecstatic because every year up until this one, we had been exiled to our maternal grandparents' home, while our house was the site of the annual New Year's Eve costume party that was inevitably the talk of the community for several days afterwards. We coughed our way through a cigarette, devoured a handful of tiny wieners, then crept back downstairs and, hiding behind the sofa in the den, watched the costumed figures arrive. Mr. Hurst showed up as

Zorro, his wife as Rapunzel, and—we thought it was so funny—the Golds appeared as Steve Lawrence and Edie Gorme, Mr. Gold in a low-cut red lamé cocktail gown and wig, Mrs. Gold with her hair slicked back, in chinos and a cardigan.

As the evening wore on and everyone got drunker, Mother and Father kept imploring us to go to bed, while their guests cajoled them into letting us stay. Eventually we were banished to our room, but that was after Barney Josephson let us each have a sip of his scotch and soda in the kitchen when no one else was around.

The next afternoon, Mother and Father insisted on dressing us up in their costumes and taking our picture. Robbie was completely lost inside of Father's clown get-up, but Mother's grass skirt and long black wig fit me perfectly. She demonstrated the hip and hand movements that are associated with Hollywood Hawaiians, and as I started to get into the groove—I was really enjoying myself—Mother said, "Very good, dear!"

I had an idea. "I'll be right back," I said. I ran upstairs and put on a t-shirt and placed two tennis balls between the cloth and my chest. Voila—tits!

As I sashayed down the stairs, hips swiveling and hands undulating, Mother squealed, "Ooo, that's good!"

But Father roared, "Yeah, TOO GOOD! Go back upstairs and change. NOW!"

The Morning After the Night Before

The first thing I remember is being startled into conscious-
ness by the telephone. My first impulse was to roll over and
pretend that I couldn't hear the piercing ring, but my effort
was stymied by the comatose body that snored loudly by my
side. I couldn't recall having invited someone over and figured
if I went back to sleep, everything would eventually fall into
place. But the phone didn't stop. It occurred to me that it might
be important, so I jumped out of bed, which was a mistake,
because my head started to reel. I had to sit down for a few
seconds. Suddenly my guest sat up and said, "Hey, Cowboy!
Aren't you gonna answer it?"

"Yeah, sure," I replied and stumbled across the room to
pick up the receiver. It was Michael.

"So, how's the mad kisser of Christopher Street today?"

"Huh?" I managed to enquire.

"I suppose you don't remember anything."

"That's a fair assessment," I mumbled.

"Do you remember when Carl showed up as Mae West?"

"No."

"Do you remember seizing his lipstick and smearing it all
over your mouth?"

"Nope."

"Well, you insisted on leaving your lip print on everyone's
left cheek."

"Did I really?"

"You most certainly did."

"Are you putting me on?"

"Hell, no!" he replied indignantly. "You made everyone pull
down their pants and you kissed all of us on our left cheek,
repainting your lips each time."

"You're kidding."

"No I'm not! Even my straight cousin from Schenectady!"

"God! I'm sorry . . . but I still can't believe it."

"Go back to sleep and call me later."

"What time is it?" I asked sheepishly.

"About four o'clock. Bye."

I hung up just as this very handsome man, with impeccable pectorals rose from my bed. "G'morning, Hotstuff." He smiled. "You sure know how to kick in the spurs and ride! Uh, which way's the john?"

I showed him the bathroom, and was putting on my robe when the doorbell rang. It was Carl, and he had apparently left Mae West at home. "I'm right on time, just like we planned. Boy, you really stole the show last night! I brought the lipstick along in case you want to do an encore." He stepped across the threshold, put down his bundles and closed the door. "Look, it was too cute to wash off. I put a Band-Aid over it when I showered." He turned around, pulled down his pants and, sure enough, there were my lips in bright scarlet. He refastened the buttons of the black Levi's and, heading for the kitchen with the packages yelled, "I hope you're hungry. I got everything from paté foie doie to smoked oysters. Champagne too!"

My stomach recoiled in terror and I decided to search for a cigarette. Super-Pecs emerged from the bathroom, winked and sprinted to the bedroom. I heard a loud popping sound and I vaguely recall sitting down on the couch when Carl came out of the kitchen with a bottle and three glasses. Just then, the hunky stranger — whom I still could not recollect meeting, let alone fucking — sauntered into the living room clutching a small mirror with six lines of coke in his right hand, and a fat joint in the other. I believe it was Carl who chimed, "Happy New Year," as we downed the first glass of bubbly, and I recall the aroma of the Columbian smoke as I accepted the joint and drew a large toke.

To be completely honest about this, I can't remember anything after that. But I can vividly recall getting to work the next morning. When I entered the reception area, Sheila stopped typing, scrutinized me from head to toe and, glancing at her watch, chided, "You are exactly seventeen and a half minutes late and you look like *death* . . . but I bet you had one helluva better time than I did!"

A Herd of Tiny Elephants

I finished listening to the life story of a stranger, and he excused himself to go to the bathroom. When the doorbell rang, Mark turned away from the circle of people with whom he had been talking and looked at me. Sylvester, his lover, sailed in from the kitchen drying his hands on his pleated, khaki slacks and signaled to Mark that he would answer it. He darted into the foyer as Mark came over to the straight-backed chair where I sat, adjacent to the small, round table bearing family photographs in gilded frames. He reached down and touched my shoulder.

"Follow me," he whispered.

"Who wouldn't?" I asked silently.

He led me down the metallic, circular staircase to the lower level and into the bedroom, a part of the duplex to which I'd never been invited. The moon cast pale yellow trapezoids on the darkened floor. He closed the drapes, the light slowly receding into black, and turned on the light. The room looked like it had been decorated for Valentine's Day. The vermillion drapes were edged with white lace, the scarlet bedspread bedecked with a pattern of hearts and flowers. Cream-colored walls were connected by a crimson trim and the gray carpet flecked with splashes of fire engine red.

He leaned against me, furtively kissed my cheeks and ran his smooth palms up and down my bare arms. I couldn't believe it was really happening. His sharp features, milky complexion and hard body beckoned to me whenever we met, but I trained myself to look without reaching out to touch.

He bit my ear and I dared to grasp the solid arms clothed in off-white raw silk. I suddenly thought of Sylvester. Surely we would be missed. Although there was a party going on, the crowd was not that large that the disappearance of one of the hosts and a guest would remain unnoticed. I was about to say that I was getting nervous, but he shushed me and began to unzip my pants.

"Hmm, no underwear. Just like I thought," he chuckled. He removed a tiny vial of coke from his pocket and sprinkled some on the part of me that lay in his hand. Stooping, he took me into his warm, wet mouth and played me like a flute concerto. After the final cadenza he zipped me up, kissed me for what seemed like a long time and said, "Let's go. I was showing you my elephants." He pointed to the bureau which supported a herd of miniature pachyderms; ebony, jade, blown glass, onyx, ivory, and marble. He picked one up. "This is Jasper." Placing it in my pocket with care, he kissed me again, turned off the light and led me back upstairs.

☆ ☆ ☆

I met Mark and Sylvester through mutual friends, Donald and Kirsten, friends of mine who lived down the street from the fashionable boutique where Sylvester worked. In spite of the difference in our sexual interests, Donald and I had become close in college and stayed in touch because of an undying interest in Jack Kerouac and Neal Cassady (actually, he wanted to *be* Kerouac and I wanted to *have* Cassady). Donald has a highly developed sense of fashion, unusual in one so hetero, and enjoyed buying clothes from well-dressed gay men. I went with him to the boutique once and sat in my t-shirt and jeans watching him model Italian slacks, English sweaters, French shirts (I suggested that we grab some tacos and catch a Fassbinder film, but he didn't make the connection). He loved discussing collars and cuffs with Sylvester and would ask for comments and suggestions. Sylvester, an average-looking guy with a small nose and thin lips, getting paunchy as he neared his late thirties, took great delight in dressing a straight man who looked like a teenybopper's heartthrob and had no qualms being around gay guys. The two became good friends and eventually introduced each other to their respective lovers.

One night Kirsten made a pot roast and invited me to dinner. She met me at the door of the small one-bedroom apartment in an untucked Oxford shirt (Donald's) and jeans, her straight blonde hair pulled up into a bun. Donald was dressed like a junior executive at his first board meeting.

The meal was wonderful and I complimented the chef. After asking if I was involved with anyone ("Not yet.") she suggested that I be introduced to her "favorite couple."

"Donald, don't you think that Joey should meet Mark and Sylvester?"

"Why?"

"They're married, right?" I asked.

"Well, yes, but they throw fabulous parties and there are always hordes of single gay guys. Have some more stringbeans. Isn't that right?"

Donald drained his wine glass. "Yup."

"How about if I invite them to dinner next week? Joey can come too and I'm sure he'll be invited to their next bash."

"Sounds great," said Donald.

"Ditto," I agreed.

I was eager to finally meet some single gay guys. It wasn't often that I met people who were interesting and also available. So I was determined to make a good impression on Mark and Sylvester.

I was the last to arrive, having had to stand in line at the bakery, waiting to purchase a pound of assorted cookies. Donald looked chic in royal blue day-glo parachute pants and a bowling shirt with Dayton, Ohio embroidered on the back and Mona, in script, over his left breast. Sylvester looked like a country squire, so neat were his sweater-vest, tweed trousers, and wing-tips. Mark, Kirsten and I wore jeans and plaids.

Donald tossed a salad, Kirsten baked lasagna, Sylvester brought champagne and Mark stuffed our noses with coke.

"This lasagna is better than my grandmother's," said Sylvester, lifting an overburdened fork.

"Tell Joey about the time you were still a dresser and had to do Ginger Rogers," suggested Donald.

Mark sighed and looked bored. Sylvester ignored him. "She was in town to appear in a benefit for the Actor's Home and someone recommended me to dress and do her hair. First of all, I had to squeeze her into a tiny frock that could barely contain her, Darling, *she's multiplying*, and her hair was so limp I figured she'd been taking it to the cleaners, *literally*, and don't you know, that woman's face has been lifted so many times, she has to look down to look up!"

Kirsten laughed so hard, she fell off her chair and almost choked on a piece of celery. I helped her up and fetched some water. She was fine a few moments later.

When we were finished eating, Donald changed the music from Vivaldi to Steely Dan, then he and Sylvester sat on the couch to discuss *Gentlemen's Quarterly*.

I helped Kirsten and Mark with the dishes. I cleared, she washed and he and I dried. He patted my ass a few times and winked at me once. We rejoined Donald and Sylvester around the coffee table, sipping and snorting, ethnic jokes bouncing from one to another. At the evening's conclusion, both Mark and Sylvester kissed me goodbye and invited me to their next soiree. It was several parties later that Mark introduced me to his little elephant friends.

☆ ☆ ☆

I was not at all pleased with the dance instructor whom I'd been over-paying for months, and Kirsten finally convinced me that we should take class together, her teacher being divine. She was right. Also, I didn't mind the trip from Sheridan Square to the Upper West Side and back; it gave me much welcomed reading time. And I got to know Kirsten a lot better. We would occasionally meet for espresso before going to class and began trading dog-eared paperbacks that each of us felt the other *had* to read. A more experienced dancer than I, she would sometimes get a part in an off-Broadway production. Both of us frequently got jobs doing small bits in Industrial Shows, usually for manufacturers of clothing or cosmetics. Between gigs she'd wait tables, walk dogs and babysit. I drove a cab.

It was about two weeks after the last party at Mark and Sylvester's. I had just gotten home from class and was leaving for work when the phone rang.

"Joey? It's Mark. How's Jasper?"

"Oh, just fine. He doesn't eat much, though."

"He'll only eat when you're not looking."

"Oh, I see. How're you, how's Sylvester?"

"Just great, we're both really fine. I called to see if you and Jasper would be available for lunch next Thursday?"

"Yes, we're very available."

"Why don't I drop by your place around noon?"

"Great!"

"Perfect."

Click.

I had to run to get to work on time. I was hailed by two hookers in mini-skirts, reeking of stale honeysuckle, their make-up looking like it had been applied by spray-can wielding graffiti artists. I picked them up at 60th and Park. Despite the loveli-

68

ness of the evening, they asked to be driven to 55th and Park. After accusing me of taking "the long way" (I knew of no other), they jumped out of the car and ran into a posh building with a doorman. For the small price of twenty-five bucks, he said, he would tell me which apartment they went to. I told him to get fucked. Later on, I picked up a middle-aged man who passed out in the back seat after giving me a Bronx address. I got him there and woke him up. He rolled out of the car, handed me a fifty (thirty-three dollar tip!) and fell asleep on the sidewalk. Typical night.

When I arrived home it must have been around 4:30. I turned on the radio, smoked a joint, and fetched Jasper from my top drawer. I turned him over in my hands and held him up to the light. Carved out of jade, he measured about an inch in height. I noticed that most of Mark's elephants had their trunks to the ground, as if grazing, but Jasper held his heavenward, as though he were about to perform a trumpet solo. Tusks defiantly thrust forward, he stood with his right legs slightly ahead of the left, his tail curving upward, frozen in mid-swing. Tiny lines had been etched on his flanks to suggest the texture of hide and the ears were so thin, they looked like they might actually flap.

When I awoke the next morning he was still clutched in the palm of my hand, bathed in sweat, but no worse for having slept with me.

☆ ☆ ☆

Upon arriving at my apartment, Mark hugged and kissed me, then stepped back to survey the space. He walked to the window and looked down at the street, turned and said, "What? No curtains?"

"Lack of disposable cash."

"How long have you been living here?" He looked disapprovingly at the stack of book-filled crates in the corner.

"Almost two years."

"And why haven't you unpacked?"

"Haven't had the time."

I invited him to sit down on my bed, which served as a couch during the day. Lighting a cigarette, he lowered himself slowly, smoothing the wrinkles in the bedspread on either side.

I turned on the radio and was about to sit down when he blurted, "I was going to suggest that we skip lunch and hang out here, but this will never do." His eyes swept my studio like a drill sergeant's, forced to rate barracks that were doomed to fail inspection.

"Are you hungry?"

"Yes," I lied.

"How about Clyde's?"

"I love it." That was true.

"Let's go then."

Somewhere between the salads and entrees we discovered that we both enjoyed the plays of Sam Shepard. Aside from that, we had little to say, much to my relief. When he asked what I thought of the fried mushrooms I said, "Delicious!"

"Wonderful . . . superb, even," he rejoined.

"Excellent," I agreed.

"The best," he exclaimed.

The two of us could trade unnecessary words and phrases until their meanings were sucked into a vortex of nonsense. Thus did I welcome the silences.

Over coffee, brandy, and cigarettes he mentioned that Sylvester would be going away for a weekend the following month.

"Would you like to come over for dinner? It would give me a chance to cook something that he doesn't like."

"How do you know *I'll* like it?"

"We can discuss it . . . I'll call you."

"Terrific."

"Wonderful."

He reached into his pocket and pulled out a small elephant of blown glass. "This is Rupert. I thought Jasper might be getting lonely. Would you mind babysitting for two of my friends?"

I smiled. "No problem. Tiny elephants don't make much noise anyway."

"Oh yes they do . . . but only when you're not around."

☆ ☆ ☆

We sat in the spacious, cluttered living room, the site of Mark and Sylvester's entertaining. Vases, of differing shapes and sizes, festooned with an equally varied selection of cut flowers, had been added to all of the familiar bric-a-brac and it felt very much like a country garden. Sylvester had gone to visit his family in Cleveland for an extended weekend and Mark invited me over to dine on endive salad and chicken au jardin, a dish that he claimed took him all day to prepare. The chicken parts, mixed together with artichoke hearts, carrots, onions, and mushrooms, were moist and tasty, easily falling from the bones. Mark, after revealing the recipe, stated that Sylvester, strictly a meat-and-potatoes person, preferred to cook meals that required as few pots and pans as possible. He, on the other hand, liked to play in the kitchen and didn't mind the cleaning up if the food turned out as he expected.

"Have you heard the latest about Kirsten and Donald?" he asked with a coy expression.

"You mean their latest fight?"

He nodded.

"Kirsten called yesterday," I sighed, "she was upset, and Donald spent the night at my place." I sipped some jasmine tea. "He was pretty upset too."

"He has a jealous nature and he must be a bit paranoid too because I know Kirsten and she would never fool around." He put down his teacup like an exclamation point.

"I think he's afraid of losing her."

"I understand that."

"Also, he *hates* his job. Imagine if you had spent as much time as he did trying to build a career as an actor and wound up a gofer for a theatrical agent."

"That's no excuse. How about some brandy?" He went to the bar and half-filled two large crystal snifters and returned. We toasted and as I lit a cigarette, he poured a huge pile of coke onto the mirror which always occupied a central position on the antique coffee table. I was impressed.

"I've never seen that much in one place at one time."

He arranged the powder into several long lines, and without looking up said, "It's a living, like any other. Except I can choose my own hours." He snorted half a line through a small glass straw and after handing it to me said, "Coke up!" I finished the line, dividing it between both nostrils, unlike Mark, who only used the one on the right because the capillaries next door had collapsed from years of abuse, as Kirsten had once said.

Moments later I felt a lightness in my brain and a half tingly, half numbing sensation spread to my hands and feet. He moved closer, started playing with my hair and rubbing my thigh. I wanted to kiss him on the lips and taste his tongue, but I was afraid to make the first move.

"How about some music?" I suggested.

"No sweat."

He walked to the stereo with an easy gait and slid a cassette into the deck. The room filled up with mellow cocktail jazz as his perfectly contoured thirty-five year old body, clothed in clinging Levi's and a ribbed, turquoise turtleneck, returned to my side. He lightly massaged my neck, kissed me and sought my tongue with his own. Our lips pressed together, we played a friendly game of hide-and-seek and I felt weightless, utterly free of gravity's pull. He drew back and did some more coke. I declined.

He removed his sweater, revealing the taut chest and stomach that I had hitherto only imagined. Unbuttoning my shirt, he unzipped my pants and stood up. I was ready to rise and follow him below to the bedroom, but he said, "I'll be right back." He went to the bathroom and came back right away with a stack of towels. After spreading them out on the thick carpet he asked me to remove the rest of my clothes and lie down. I stretched out on my back. He fetched a tray with small bottles and selected one with an amber fluid. "Smell this." He passed it under my nose and the scent of some unidentifiable wild flower engulfed me. Pouring some into his palm, he oiled my arms and chest, then my thighs and calves. He admonished me to roll over onto my stomach and worked it into my neck, shoulders and back. I started to groan and writhe, his firm touch sending me into spasms of sensation. He worked his way down to my buttocks, the backs of my legs, the soles of my feet. He dried his hands and replenished the brandy snifters. "I'll be right back . . . don't go away!" He went to the bathroom and came back immediately, apparently forgetting to turn off the tap; the sound of running water tainted the music. He told me to roll over onto my back. Bending down, he placed one arm under my neck, the other beneath my knees and lifted me, cradling me like an infant. When was he going to get to the sexual part? I wondered while I was carried to the bathroom and gently placed in the tub, half full of warm water. I was bathed and then shampooed with some greenish gel that smelled like juniper. He towelled me dry from head to feet and combed my hair.

We returned to the couch, I completely naked, he, still in his jeans. He pulled a thick joint from his cigarette pack, lit it and passed it. I began to feel a little dizzy after the third toke.

"Shall we go down?"

I shook my head.

When he turned on the light I thought I was hallucinating. All of the reds were gone. The carpet was the color of astroturf, the curtains a satiny chartreuse, the bedspread a salad of cucumbers, avocadoes, and limes in free-fall. The elephants grazed silently on the bureau. He finally stripped.

"Love the new decor," I said, referring to his naked body.

"We change it from time to time," he gestured at the drapes.

We got in between the cool sheets and held each other for a while.

"Are you tired?"

"A little," I lied. Spaced out would be a far more accurate description.

"So am I. Go to sleep, Joey, my pretty little . . . what does one call a male ballerina?"

"A dancer!"

That was the first and only time that I ever had the last word; he fell asleep before he could respond.

In the morning I had to leave early to warm up for an audition. Mark stayed in bed while I let myself out. Later that night I was going through the pocket of my denim jacket and found a small jeweler's box. Inside was a tiny elephant, obsidian I think, with a small card attached to its trunk that said, "Hi, my name is Cicero, what's yours?"

☆ ☆ ☆

Two weeks later I called Mark and Sylvester to say hello and see how they were. Sylvester answered the phone.

"Hello? Sylvester? This is Joey."

"Oh. Hello. I suppose you want to speak to Mark."

"Well, not necessarily, I just wanted to say 'hi'."

"He's not here right now, I'll tell him you called." He slammed the receiver down.

Did he suspect that I had seen Mark while he was away? I wasn't certain. Perhaps he was in a foul mood.

Later that week, however, I was in the lobby of a movie theater with Donald and Kirsten. We were going to see *My Dinner With Andre*. They had greeted me a bit coolly, I thought, but didn't say anything. I returned from the concession stand with a coke and was about to share the good news that I'd gotten a call-back on my audition when Donald blurted, "How *could* you?"

"How could I what?"

Kirsten interjected, "Are you having an affair with Mark?"

"No."

"Are you sleeping together?"

73

"We did, once. What's the big deal . . . and how did you know?"

"Well, Sylvester told us," said Kirsten.

"How did *he* find out?"

"Mark told him. He tells him *everything*," said Donald.

"Oh yeah? What's *everything*?"

"Jasper, Rupert, and Cicero," they said as if they'd rehearsed it.

We never did see the film. Kirsten stated that although she would never do it herself, it was okay, in principle, for two people who had been living together for a while to fool around. Donald disagreed. He insinuated that Kirsten had a secret lover stashed away somewhere and before I knew it, they were screaming at each other. I got them out of the theater. Kirsten hailed a cab and Donald and I took the subway. He crashed on the floor at my studio that night.

☆ ☆ ☆

Mark called, he caught me at home between class and work, and asked if I would be interested in seeing Sam Shepard's *Buried Child*, dinner afterwards, with he and Sylvester. I questioned the wisdom of such a move. Wasn't Sylvester, after all, angry with me? Mark suggested that if the three of us had a good time together, the wound might heal faster.

When we met, Sylvester greeted me warmly, but grumbled to Mark throughout the production, Shepard plays not being his favorite entertainment. Glitzy Broadway musicals were more suited to his taste. Mark and I loved it, though.

We went to eat at Blue Skies and everything was very good. The pasta was not overcooked, the escargots buttery and well-garlicked, and the pianist-singer was actually quite pleasant.

When the waiter placed the check face down on the table, Mark immediately snatched it and reached for his wallet. I took out mine as well.

"How much do I owe for the theater and dinner?"

"Nothing," said Mark.

I looked at Sylvester, bewildered.

"Come on now, how much was the ticket?"

"I'm not telling. It was a gift. Please accept it."

I looked at Sylvester again. He stared ahead blankly.

"Okay, I accept, thank you. Now, how much is my part of the bill?"

74

"It's on me."

"Nope. I'd really like to pay my own way. Please let me see it," I indicated the check, trying to hide my embarrassment.

"No!"

Sylvester came to my rescue. "He wants to pay for his dinner. Let him."

"No . . . it's on me."

"You give him elephants, cocaine, and your body, and now you want to feed him?"

I wished I could click my heels and disappear.

"What I do with my boyfriends is none of your business."

"Wait a minute," I said, "I'm not your boyfriend."

Sylvester smiled. "According to Mark, you two have been carrying on like sodomy was just invented."

"That's not true! We spent one night together and we didn't even do anything."

"Liar!" spat Mark. He placed a one hundred dollar bill on the table and walked out.

I looked at Sylvester. "I swear, we had one date and nothing happened!"

"Oh, I know . . . don't worry about it. This is the fourth and last time he's tried to convince me that he was having a torrid love affair with a younger guy. It feeds his vanity. And I'm fed up."

We left the restaurant and Sylvester signaled a taxi. He hugged me and said goodbye, leaving me on the curb. I started to walk home, fingering the tissue paper wrapped around the miniature mammals in my pocket. They were quiet and still. I had intended to return them to the herd, but Mark's sudden departure and subsequent silence prevented my doing so.

A few weeks later, Kirsten left Donald and moved in with the guy whom she had denied she was seeing. "He's a dancer," she eventually confided, "the only straight one in the Greater Metropolitan Area."

Shortly thereafter, Sylvester moved out of Mark's duplex and roomed with Donald until he found a place of his own.

I resolved to never again get involved with a married man. The potential for touchy situations is too great, the opportunities for getting hurt and causing pain, too numerous. Besides, who wants to be a training wheel on a sixteen-speed racer?

Jasper, Rupert, and Cicero get along very well together and have comfortably settled in on the night table by my bed.

Their food budget is easily within my grasp. They clean up after themselves. If they make any noise it's only when I'm out of hearing range. And if they ever have sex, I've not been around to catch them at it.

Gang Of Five

1

Joel and Gerry sat in Professor DeFranco's History class and exchanged glances of boredom. The old fart was going on and on about Abelard and Heloise and concluded the lecture by saying, ". . . and so Abelard paid for his so-called crime by having the thing with which he did his wrongness cut off." He leered and frowned. "Read chapter twelve for the next time. Class dismissed."

Gerry, short and thin, with hair that looked like it had been styled with an egg-beater, stood up and whispered in Joel's ear, "Hey, I just scored some red Lebanese. You wanna try some?"

"You gotta ask?" Joel reached for the cigarette pack in his faded work shirt. He lit one and exhaled a large plume of smoke. They were making their way out of the old brownstone on Beacon Street when they were waylaid by Chip.

"Joel, it's here. I was sorting the mail this morning, and you got it."

Joel glanced at Chip's crotch, then raised his eyes. "What?"

"Those records from the Columbia Record Club."

"What's he talkin' about?" asked Gerry, crossing his arms over his thin chest.

"You know those ads where you join a record club and get ten free albums for a buck?"

"Yeah."

"Well, I joined. As Joe Nobody."

"No shit," said Gerry. "What d'ja get?"

"A bunch of weird junk," said Chip.

Joel grimaced at Chip, noted his muscular thighs, and said, "Well, I figured if I was gonna get some free albums, I'd get stuff that I wouldn't ordinarily buy. You know, explore around a little."

On the top floor of the boys' dormitory, in the room that had been dubbed "The Penthouse," Gerry was breaking up hash into his stone pipe, Chip was admiring his biceps and pectorals in the mirror and Joel was opening the large package.

"Far fuckin' out. Brand new music for my hungry ears."

Searching for a book of matches, Gerry said, "Are you ever gonna tell me what you got?"

"For starters, there's *Brilliant Corners* by Thelonius Monk."

"Who?"

"Thelonius Monk. Jazz pianist."

"Oh."

"Then there's *Tammy Wynette's Greatest Hits, Volume I*."

"The country singer?"

"Yes."

"How bizarre."

"And *La Mer* by Debussy."

"All right, I get the picture. No rock, huh?"

"No Hendrix, no Cream, no James Gang, no Stones, just crap," said Chip.

"Not even any Band or Small Faces?" asked Gerry with mock incredulity.

"Nope. Brand new tunes for jaded goons."

Gerry lit the pipe, took a large drag and passed it to Chip, who sat on the bed. Joel placed a record on the spindle and touched the automatic switch. He sat on the floor and took the pipe. The three of them looked at each other as the intro to "Stand By Your Man" filled the room. They passed the pipe around several times and by the song's conclusion, they were somewhere between Jupiter and Uranus.

"Interesting," said Gerry, staring at the picture on the album cover.

"Too weird," said Chip, crossing his legs.

"Far out," said Joel, noting the way that Chip's stomach never bulged out over his jeans, even when sitting.

Tammy Wynette was halfway through "Apartment #9" when Gerry began to refill the pipe. Joel rose to change the record and cued up Thelonius Monk. When he sat down, he felt the rush from the smoke. He glanced at Chip's pretty-boy face and the halo effect of his golden curls. As was his habit when stoned, Joel's mind wandered through his memory.

He could remember his first day in Boston. It was the beginning of orientation week, and when his parents deposited him and his belongings at the dormitory on Beacon Street, he had at first tried to be brave. As soon as they were out of sight, however, he felt a slight choking in his throat, and a rush of nostalgia for the small, suburban town he had been so desperate to leave. He unpacked slowly, hoping that his roommate would materialize so they could meet, but finding the task completed and having nothing else to do, he decided to take a stroll and explore the immediate vicinity. When he had walked down the six flights of stairs and emerged onto the street, he saw many young people saying good-bye to their parents.

A pretty girl with long, black hair stood on the corner of Beacon and Berkeley, smoking a joint with a guy whose hair looked Dylanesque. Joel walked past and they smiled. He smiled back, but quickly walked on, unsure in the light of such friendliness. He had heard that the big city was tough and cruel and had prepared himself for it. But these people seemed nice. "I've got a lot to learn," he said to himself.

Heading up Berkeley Street toward Commonwealth Avenue, he passed staid brownstones that seemed to harbor ancient secrets. Cars went whizzing by and strangers came toward him, mostly youthful, all looking very hip. The faded jeans and long hair made him realize that his chinos and semi-crewcut would have to go if he was going to fit in. It was like getting out of prison. His parents, whom he jokingly referred to sometimes as "the wardens," would never let him dress like the other kids. But now he had his chance. He smiled inwardly and lit a cigarette.

He walked on, lost in thought, occasionally distracted by a passerby or an odd building, when he came to a large park he later found out was called "the Common." He passed a small lake with boats shaped like swans. Sitting down on a bench, he lit another cigarette and leaned back. A young couple came over, placed their jackets on the bench and proceeded to dance. Not like in a ballroom or discotheque, but choreography such as a chorus line might do. It looked like they were rehearsing for a stage production of some sort, when out of nowhere, a drunk appeared, staggered over to the dancers and attempted to join in. They were doing high kicks, first to the left and then to the right, when the derelict fell on his ass. The dancers laughed, gathered their things, said goodbye and departed. He applauded their effort and waved.

Stamping out the cigarette, he stood up and began walking again, when a middle-aged gentleman accosted him. "Excuse me, can you tell me how to get to Washington Street?"

"I'm sorry, Sir, but I'm new in town and have no idea."

The stranger eyed him up and down. "I've never been to Boston before either. Where are you from?"

"New York. Actually, Long Island. I'm just starting college. Well, I hope you find Washington Street."

Joel turned to walk away.

"Wait a minute. Perhaps you can still help."

"What do you mean?" asked Joel.

"Would you be interested in, possibly, I mean, do you ever think about sex?"

Joel blushed. "What are you, some kind of pimp?"

"No, no, you've got it all wrong. Why don't you come over to my hotel room and we can discuss it?"

Joel never ran that fast in his life. He ran until he could not go on, and turned to make sure he had not been followed. Plopping down on the grass, he held his head in his hands until the labored breathing began to subside. "Goddamn," he said to himself. He had always hated the overprotectiveness of his parents and the isolation of the suburbs. If he had grown up in a city he would have the street smarts to recognize an old queer on the make. He hated himself for his naivete and for handling the situation so awkwardly.

He was walking back to the dormitory when he saw the pretty girl again and crossed the street so he could smile at her when he passed by. She surprised him by introducing herself. "Hi, my name's Martha, what's yours?"

"Joel."

"You want to smoke a joint?"

"Sure."

They walked down Beacon Street toward Kenmore Square, talking about the Rolling Stones. He didn't really care for them, but did not want her to know that, so he pretended to be a big fan. "Yeah, I saw them at the Forest Hills Tennis Stadium a few years ago. I think Jagger's fantastic," he lied.

"I grew up in Forest Hills."

"Really? I'm from New York too."

They played the game of "Do You Know?" and when they realized they had no friends or acquaintances in common, they turned and walked back. The young man with tousled hair whom Martha had been with earlier came over to them and she introduced him as Gerry. They shook hands and Gerry asked Joel if he wanted to buy a hit of orange sunshine.

"No thanks," said Joel, "maybe some other time. I'm gonna go back to the dorm and see if my roommate checked in yet. Take care."

As Joel turned and walked away, Martha swallowed the bright orange pill that Gerry had placed in the palm of her hand.

Climbing the six flights up, Joel passed room after room with chattering young men — some preppy, some hippy — and reflected on a conversation he had with his best friend back home. He prayed that his roommate would be anything but a jock. He cautiously turned the key in the lock and found a body stretched out on the lower berth of the bunk beds. Jumping up in surprise was a guy wearing only his jockey shorts. He looked like a model. Sculpted body, chiselled features, curly blond hair and green eyes, the color of pistachio ice-cream.

"Hi, I'm Chip."

Joel detected a mid-western accent. "My name's Joel. I'm from New York. Yourself?"

"Indiana. I see you play guitar. Mind if I look at it?"

"No. I sing and write songs, too. You play?" Joel tried to keep his eyes from Chip's perfect torso.

"The only thing I play is football. I was team captain last year."

"No shit."

"Yeah, but my main hobby is girls."

He chuckled and playfully punched Joel's arm. Sitting back down on the bed he sighed and added, "Ah yes, girls. Can't live without 'em."

"You mind if I play a record?"

"Not at all. Nice stereo. What have you got?" asked Chip, twirling a gold curlicue around his index finger.

"Oh, a little of everything. What do you want to hear?"

"Anything."

Deciding to play it safe, Joel extracted *Rubber Soul* by the Beatles and played side two at a moderate volume. He sat down in the chair near the window and asked Chip what subject he planned to major in.

"I have no idea and couldn't care less. You?"

"Well, I really want to be a musician, but to be realistic, I'm gonna go for a B.A. in English Literature and maybe I'll minor in Education and teach."

81

Chip bounded from the bed and lit a cigarette. He pulled a trunk out from under the bed, opened it, and took out a rolled-up poster. "It's Hendrix. Mind if I put it up on the wall over here?"

"Go ahead. Nice colors."

"Hendrix is so cool it's scary. You got any pot?"

"No, but I was thinking of buying some. Maybe we could split a lid?" Joel attempted to pry his eyes from Chip's thighs and calves.

"Great. You hungry?"

"Yeah," said Joel, looking away.

"I'm starved. Why don't we go over to the cafeteria and check out the grub?"

"Sure."

Chip put on a plaid shirt, tight faded jeans and sneakers. Reaching for his Varsity jacket, he checked himself in the mirror, and finding the image flawless said, "Let's go."

They walked slowly down the street and Chip pointed out the attractive women. He had a comment for every female that passed by. Some were too old, too fat or too cheap-looking. But every now and then he would say, "Wow, I could go for that." Joel just sort of agreed with everything, but it was more in the spirit of being friendly than any actual similarity of opinion.

They stood in line with trays and accepted the overcooked food. It did not look very appetizing. They finally found places to sit, opposite one another at the end of a long table. Chip attacked his food, while Joel tasted it with apprehension. He decided he was less hungry than he thought. Looking past Chip, he noticed Martha and Gerry sitting two tables away. He noted that they could not take their eyes away from each other.

"What are you staring at?" asked Chip.

"Oh, these people I met before. Martha and Gerry, two tables behind you."

As Chip looked around, Martha smiled at Joel. He nodded back. "I could go for that," said Chip, hitching his thumb toward Martha. "I'm gonna get some more milk. You want any?"

Joel was startled from his reverie of the past when a pack of Bambu smacked his cheek and landed in his lap. Chip ginned and laughed. "Hey, why don't you roll us a joint? I'm gonna put on some *real* music." Chip sprang to his feet and moved to the stereo. Joel sighed as he watched Chip's tightly jeaned ass flex right, left, right, left in syncopated rhythm. He spilled some grass onto a album cover and rolled a hefty joint. Licking it, he sighed again as Chip sat down. Joel looked down at his own body, boyish and undefined, glanced at Gerry's anorexic frame, then ogled Chip's athletically tapered torso. He lit the joint, passed it to Gerry and tried to imagine having sex with Chip, as Deep Purple shot out of the twin speakers.

2

Thoreau College was a small, private institution, located in the Back Bay area of Boston. Most of the school's buildings were on Beacon Street, one block away from the scenic Charles River. Dividing the metropolitan area into two distinct camps — Boston and Cambridge — the river snaked it's way between the sister cities, with long, slender strip parks running parallel to the polluted water. The park on the Boston side was called the Esplanade, and it was there that the Thoreau students would go on warm, sunny days to study or get high. At night, the Esplanade served as a cruising area for the many gay students that had emigrated to the city of schools for either educational or recreational fulfillment.

While it was clear to Joel that Chip's main pursuit was women and Gerry's principle hobby was drugs, Joel was uncertain about himself. He felt divided. No longer a child, but not yet an adult, interested in learning, but eager to experience the pleasure he had been denied while growing up. He was torn between furthering his education and satisfying his lust for men. At an early age he'd known he was gay, but was unable to explore this facet of life while living at his parents' home. Besides, the small, suburban town offered no apparent opportunities.

Suddenly, he'd been thrust into a living situation that seemed to mock everything he'd known until then. His dormitory was packed with horny, young guys, much like himself. And though a handful were unquestionably gay, many of the others were more than willing to experiment. And the presence of certain drugs in the bloodstream only diminished some people's already lax inhibitions. Joel had become infatuated with Chip's body, but Chip was so obsessed with women that Joel was terrified of even suggesting any kind of physical involvement. Still, the sight of Chip naked always made him erect.

Joel thumbed through *Rolling Stone* while Chip occupied the bathroom. He came across an article on aging blues singer

Son House and chuckled at the glaring inaccuracies. When he heard the toilet flush, he put the magazine away and cued up his Robert Johnson album. When Chip emerged, blowing his nose into a tissue, Joel turned up the volume, entered the bathroom and shut the door. Chip laughed to himself, thinking that Joel couldn't even take a shit without listening to his old blues records.

Meanwhile, Joel's cock was on fire. He had stumbled upon the secret of masturbation while very young, and had become addicted to the feeling. But as he had grown older, he feared that he might be making moaning noises at the crucial moment, and usually indulged himself only when his parents and sister were away. Even then, he'd fallen into the habit of playing loud music and running the shower to conceal any sound that might result from his clandestine activity. When he had gotten to college he did not care who heard what, but he retained the old habits.

The sweet anticipation was over. Anointing himself with Vaseline, he stepped into the shower stall. His thighs took up the pulsating Mississippi Delta rhythm. Letting his thoughts roam freely over Chip's well-contoured body, he closed his eyes tightly and worked himself until his loins tightened and he reached ecstatic release. He opened his eyes, shook out the last few drops and soaped himself all over. After showering, he emerged, still toweling himself dry.

"You sure take a lot of showers," said Chip.

"You noticed, huh?"

☆ ☆ ☆

Martha and Gerry had begun to hang out together on their first day in Boston. At first, their relationship centered around their mutual interest in drugs. One day, after a few weeks into the first semester, he had invited her to spend the night in his room at the boys' dorm. His roommate, a nerdy guy whom he referred to as "Poindexter" to his friends, had gone home for the weekend.

Martha, wearing a flamingoed caftan, lounged on the bed eating Oreos while Gerry sat at his desk studying a Mass Communications text. She got up and walked over to the bookshelf, selected a volume of William Blake's poetry and returned to the bed. Her silky, dark hair, parted in the middle, flowed down the sides of her face to her breasts. She had barely begun to read when Gerry turned the stereo on, boogied over to the bed and sat down beside her. Putting the book on the floor, she pulled herself up to get next to him and allowed her breast to rub against him. Clad in a dashiki with concentric diamonds outlined in tan, black and white, he touched her cheek. She ran her fingers through his bushy hair and whispered, "Hi there, cutie."

"Let's get high," he said. "I got some new stuff and it's better than purple haze. Wanna check it out?"

"Does the Pope shit in the woods?" she said, checking her hair for split ends. He broke the small tablet in half, reached for the coke can on the night table, and handed the acid and soda pop to her. He waited until she had swallowed hers, then took his and tapped a joint out of his cigarette pack. "This oughta send us merrily on our way."

They passed the joint back and forth ever so slowly. Staring into space, they took deep hits and exhaled cumulus billows of aromatic Colombian smoke. The reefer and record ended simultaneously and she blurted, "Can we hear Carole King now?"

"You really want to listen to that wimpy shit?"

"Yes."

"All right, but then we gotta hear Hendrix or something equally quintessential."

"What's fair is fair. Kiss me?"

He pecked her on the cheek and got up to change the disc.

They had actually fallen in love with each other a few days before, but neither was really aware of how the other felt. Although they hadn't had real sex yet, they had made out a few times.

The acid started to kick in and they lay in each others arms, indulging their private fantasies. "What are you thinking about?" he asked.

"If you really want to know I'll tell you, but it's dumb."

"Tell me anyway."

"I'm moving through space," she began. "Completely tripped out, hurtling through the cosmos. My body feels light and supple. I can smell gardenias and patchouli. There are asteroids and meteors racing by. It looks like there's going to be a collision every second, but it all seems to work out just in time. My skin feels all tingly and you feel like you're a part of me. I mean, I feel like a part of you. You know what I mean. I feel like I'm sailing in outer space and it's never gonna stop. I don't want it to. It feels too good."

There was silence. The record player had turned itself off

and except for the faint sounds from the street that penetrated the window pane, it was very quiet.

"Your turn. Where are you?"

"Somewhere in a jungle. Probably Africa. It's dark except for this enormous bonfire. Black natives are dancing around it. There's a million conga drums tapping out rhythms. I feel like I'm vibrating to the beat. I can smell ganja and taste exotic liqueurs that no white man has ever tried before. A short distance away, there's an orgy. A swirl of arms and legs and the smell of sweat. I'm dancing around the fire and every time I pass the writhing bodies I'm tempted to join in, but I haven't yet."

"Why not?"

"Chicken, I guess."

"You won't know if you like it or not unless you try it," she said. He kissed her on the lips. Their tongues met. Gerry hugged her tighter and her breath grew short. They held to each other tightly as he explored the interior of her mouth.

"Are we gonna do it?" he asked.

"Yes."

"Wanna smoke another joint first?"

"Sure. Anything. Can we hear Carole King now?"

"Of course. I'm an easy guy to get along with," he grinned.

"Shut up and kiss me."

He was happy to comply. He lit another joint and passed it to her. Martha placed the fiery end in her mouth and gave him a shotgun. Receiving the joint, he did the same for her. Then she inhaled a huge cloud of smoke, told him to exhale, and blew the smoke into his mouth. His face lit up. "What a great idea," he said and returned the same cloud of smoke to her waiting mouth.

He tentatively undressed her, very slowly, as though she might be an infant in swaddling. She stroked the fine hairs that sprouted from his bony chest. He cupped her rounded, but smallish breasts in his hands and felt them all around. Taking her left breast into his mouth, Gerry sucked at her nipple like a toothless baby. Martha let her hand slide along his slender thigh as she felt for the warm bulge encased in briefs. When she touched the mound of his flaccid, curled up cock, it began to pulsate and grow. Their breathing quickened as their tongues met in midair and they fell back on the comforter in a tight embrace. He removed the stiff dashiki and they both wriggled out of their underwear.

86

Martha sighed and stroked his cheek. Taking his cock in her warm hands, she leaned over and flicked the tip with her tongue. Gerry arched his back and moaned. He began to writhe uncontrollably, surrounded by her mouth like an arrow in a quiver. He pulled out slowly and lay her on her back, showering her face with wet kisses. Their mouths locked and their tongues fought as he eased his full weight onto her. Martha, in a frenzy, took hold of him and guided him into her. She felt a thousand tiny electrical sparks igniting inside, and a million shooting stars ricocheted through her mind. With deep but gentle thrusts, Gerry established an accelerating rhythm pattern that soon erupted into volcanic cataclysm. She screamed and bit his ear.

They slowed and stopped. They kissed. Their eyes conversed silently as they lay side by side on the damp sheet.

☆ ☆ ☆

As soon as they'd entered the room, Chip locked the door and checked his wristwatch. Forty-five minutes to go. Nancy threw her coat on the bed and sighed, "It's too hot in here."

Chip flung the window open. "We can't control the heat from here. The thermostat is in the basement, where the house director lives, and it's always cold down there. So we sweat and he freezes."

Nancy, a tall girl with large breasts and brown hair styled in a page-boy, checked her make-up in the mirror. She erased a smudge of lipstick with the end of her pinky.

"Come over here and sit down," said Chip.

She swivelled to the bed and sat down. Chip put his arm around her shoulder and kissed her.

"What's the rush?" she pulled away.

Chip glanced at his wristwatch. "My roommate will be back in exactly thirty-seven minutes. It's the only class he always goes to."

"I get it," she said, unbuttoning her blouse. Chip leaped out of his own clothing and hastily unhooked her bra. She wriggled out of her slacks and panties and Chip, already hard, lay down on top of her and started pumping.

"Take it easy."

"Sorry."

He ground his hips up and down, while keeping an eye on the watch, poised for viewing just beyond her field of vision.

"You're gonna take me out one of these nights?" she gasped.

"Uh huh."

His motion accelerated and sweat formed on his brow. Her back arched up and he dug deeply. A shudder ran through his body as he exploded, moaning at peak volume.

"Shh," she cautioned. "You'll wake the dead."

"Uh, sorry," he said.

He rolled off of her. "Gee, uh, Nancy, that was great." He looked at his wristwatch. Eleven minutes. "Why don't we get dressed and go for some coffee?"

She slipped her arms through the straps of her bra. "Hey, big spender, do you think you can afford it," she said, as sarcastically as she dared.

"Gee, I think so," he said, pretending not to notice.

He locked the door behind them with three and a half minutes to spare.

3

Martha's dormitory was located a few blocks south of the boys' dorm on Commonwealth Ave. Presided over by Miss Allerton, a heavy-set woman with sagging breasts, the building was older and more ornate than its male counterpart. And the rules for the girls were much more strict. Although the boys could come and go as they pleased and were allowed female guests, the girls had curfews and males were not permitted beyond the reception desk where Miss Allerton kept watch.

Martha's roommate, Jacqui, was a short, lithe black girl with an Afro hairdo, high cheekbones and wistful eyes. Jacqui and Martha had become friends immediately, but at first did not spend much time together because Jacqui was more interested in poetry than drugs. She ignored her class schedule and spent most of her time at the school library reading her favorite modern poets. When the library closed she returned to her room and wrote poems of her own.

A few weeks after arriving in Boston, she'd sent off a poem she'd written called "Black Mama," a rambling meditation on black American women. The poem had been accepted by a literary journal published at Boston University. Elated at the prospect of seeing her first poem in print, she began to spend more time with Martha and eventually learned about the pleasure to be had getting high. She was eager to meet "The Guys."

So Martha organized a picnic at the Esplanade to celebrate the arrival of spring.

They spread blankets on the grass, placed the food in the shade of a sprawling tree and smoked a couple of joints. Gazing at the sailboats and skiffs that moved back and forth on the waters of the Charles, they listened to rock music on a transistor radio. Chip suddenly jumped up and declared, "It's frisbee time!"

Everyone except for Joel got to their feet and ran to a clearing. Reaching for his book, Joel turned the radio off, stretched himself out on an aqua blanket and turned to chapter seven of *Daniel Deronda* by George Eliot. He was absorbed in his reading, mesmerized by the coquetry of Gwendolyn Harleth, when he was distracted by the voice of a child who had wandered over to where he lay. He looked up and grinned just as the toddler's mother came along to apologize and whisk the youngster away.

Having finished chapter seven, Joel debated the wisdom of starting the next one, not wanting to be interrupted in the middle. He unpacked his guitar and strummed a few chords. Then the hungry frisbee players pounced on him, shrieking with laughter. Jacqui proceeded to open a bottle of wine while Gerry foraged for a fig newton. Martha crumbled some hash into a well-resined pipe. She lit it and passed it to Jacqui who took a small hit, passed the pipe and filled five paper cups with rosé. Students and teachers wandered by as the sun glittered through the leaves of the overhanging tree, casting shifting jewels on the grass.

"Martha said you just got a poem published," said Gerry.

Jacqui nodded. "My first."

"I understand you write a lot."

"It's the only thing that really interests me."

"Shit," said Chip, "I hate poetry. It's too hard to understand." He turned the radio on. "Wordsworth and Longfellow and all those guys make me sick."

"Me too," said Jacqui. "Irrelevant ranting and raving. I prefer poetry rendered in modern language."

"You mean, like Rod McKuen?" asked Gerry, sarcastically.

"Who's Rod McKuen?" asked Chip.

"Forget it," said Joel with a superior air. He looked at Jacqui. "How do you like living in the dormitory?"

"It's almost like a prison, but Miss Allerton is okay. I can live with it."

"I prefer the boys' dorm," said Martha. She winked at Gerry. "It's much cozier than Miss Allerton's Internment Camp for Young Girls."

"You mean women," said Jacqui.

"Right, women," said Martha. "I have to forge a note from my mother saying I'm going home for the weekend every time I sleep over with Gerry."

The bottle of rosé and baggies of dope emptied as the five stomachs were filled with cheese, bread and fruit. As the sun began its descent, the gang packed up the remains, folded the blankets, and headed back to their respective dormitories.

☆ ☆ ☆

Halfway through the second semester, Chip had noticed a girl hanging around school, and her grace and loneliness completely overwhelmed him. While most of the female students were fairly adolescent in their appearance and behavior, she had the air of a sophisticated woman. He wasted no time trying to meet her and asked for a date. Her name was Genevieve and she readily agreed to have dinner with him. They started dating regularly, and Chip was so proud to be seen with her that at first he didn't mind that she wasn't willing to put out. He was certain that she was interested. She would flirt shamelessly in public, but always parried his quests for satisfaction when they were alone. Chip, to alleviate his horniness, would occasionally fuck some other girl who desired him, but he always felt above these easy conquests. He eventually grew tired of bestowing his favors on underlings while his entire allowance was squandered on Genevieve's expensive tastes.

One afternoon, Chip's libido got the best of him and he had a boisterous argument with Genevieve on the sidewalk in front of the Student Union building. Martha happened to be sitting on a stoop across the street, trying to memorize some lines for her Voice and Articulation class. When Chip stormed away from Genevieve with a look of defeat, Martha intercepted his path. "Can I buy you a cup of coffee?"

"Sure. Why not? Take pity on the miserable."

"Cheer up. You can tell me all about it."

They walked slowly towards the coffee shop down the street. Martha chatted about nonsensical trivia in an effort to distract him. It worked. When they sat down at a small table for two, he was relaxed enough to talk about his problem rationally.

"So," began Martha, stirring sugar into her coffee, "she's a real cockteaser, huh?"

"Yeah. Fuckin' bitch. Playin' with my head. I've got a lot to learn."

"Don't say that. It's not your fault. Don't blame yourself for her shortcomings. You're an attractive guy. Women will always find you desirable and you can do a lot better than stuck-up, snotty Genevieve."

"You really think so?"

"I know it."

"I guess I set my sights too high."

"Au contraire. You were deceived by a wolf in sheep's clothing. It can happen to anyone."

"Yeah . . . thanks . . . you're right . . . I was too involved to see what was happening . . . shit . . . I'm such a fool . . . okay . . . I'm over it . . . don't want to bore you . . . let's change the subject."

"All right."

"Sorry I couldn't make it to see your play. How did it go?"

Martha sipped her coffee and gazed at Chip's radiant eyes. "Great. I loved doing it. The character I played says and does things that I never get to do or say in real life. I got a lot off my chest. Good therapy. The audience seemed to like it and my drama Prof. complimented me. I guess it was successful. You know, while we're on the subject, you know a lot more about me than I do about you. Like, for example, what do you want to do?"

"What do you mean?"

"You know, with your life? Your career? I mean, I want to be an actress and Gerry wants to direct films. What about you?"

"Well," he confessed, twirling a blond curlicue around his index finger, "I have this fantasy that I want to be an actor."

"Why don't you take any acting classes?"

"You're gonna think this is stupid, but here goes. I want to be discovered. I want to just have a regular job and have somebody look at me one day and say, 'Hey kid, I'm gonna make you a star.' You know, like Lana Turner. Or better yet, Mark Frechette. One day he's walking down Charles Street and Antonioni is driving by in a limo and the next thing you know, he's starring in *Zabriskie Point*."

"That's quite a romantic and far-fetched notion," She pulled her hair from her shoulders and flung it back. "The chances of that ever happening are very remote."

91

"That's what makes it so attractive. It's a real longshot. It may never pay off, but if it does, I'll be immortal."

"Good luck," she said with a sigh. "I guess anything is possible."

"You mean, *everything* is possible."

☆ ☆ ☆

The hip, long-haired English teacher, Mr. Blakely, talked about the Black Mountain school of poetry. He went on and on about Charles Olson and Robert Creeley, completely unaware that the class would much rather be discussing the Beats or the significance of poetry in rock lyrics. Jacqui and Joel sat in back of the classroom and pretended they were taking notes on the lecture.

"Jacqui," he wrote, "you've gotta do it. It's an opportunity to communicate your thoughts to other people. You work so hard on your poems. What's the use if nobody reads them or hears them? To write just for yourself is Literary Masturbation."

"Joel," she wrote back, "this is no ordinary poetry reading. All of us are black lesbians. I'm not into pigeonholes. Besides, I'm not ready for the world at large to find out my little secret. It's okay that the gang knows. But it's not something I'm ready to advertise."

The class was dismissed and they could talk.

"Does Martha know you're a lesbian?"

"Of course."

"She never said anything about it."

"Why should she?"

"I don't know." He touched Jacqui's arm. "I'm gay, but I haven't said anything yet to Chip or Gerry."

"What are you afraid of?"

"I'm not sure."

"Well then," she said triumphantly, "that settles it. I'm definitely going to participate in the reading."

"Great. What changed your mind?"

"You and your uptight attitude. If there's one gay person at the reading who is able to feel more secure about herself after hearing me read, it will be worth it."

"Can I come?"

"I'd love to have you there, Joel, but it's for black lesbians only."

"Oh, I see."

"Maybe someday we won't have to have so many restrictions."

"Yeah, I hope so," he said.

☆ ☆ ☆

It was a warm spring evening, and Chip sat on his bed smoking a joint. He decided to turn the radio on. The mellifluous voice of Eric Jackson smoothly segued from Little Feat to Fairport Convention on WBCN, the reigning free-form rock station. Opening a box of animal crackers, he began to chew on a sweet rhino when Jackson cut the song short and announced, "Police urge all citizens to avoid Harvard Square, as the antiwar demonstration has erupted into violence. Again, Harvard Square is off-limits until further notice. Now, back to the music."

That was all Chip needed to hear. He grabbed his keys and was out the door seconds later, forgetting to turn off the radio and extinguish the light. Flagging down a taxi was easy and he instructed the driver to take him to Harvard Square, "the sooner, the better."

The car crossed over to Cambridge via the Massachusetts Avenue Bridge and he commanded the driver to let him off a few blocks south of the square. There were police everywhere. Students were running around in a thousand directions and several overturned cars were engulfed in flames. He was trying to get the sense of what was happening, when a tear gas canister exploded a few yards away. He was instantly overwhelmed by the billowy fumes and began to cough. A voice from out of nowhere shouted *"Come with us!"*

The next thing he was aware of was racing down Dunster Street with a man and a woman on either side of him. The three ducked into an old clapboard house after running for several blocks. The interior was cluttered with potted plants, drug paraphernalia and dozens of cats. The couple offered Chip the use of the bathroom. He washed his face and waited for his heart to stop pounding. When he emerged, his rescuers offered him mu tea, raisins and Screaming Yellow Zonkers.

Chip tried to talk like a revolutionary. "We've got to make our feelings known. Just 'cause we're students they think we don't have anything to say, or have the right to express it. Meanwhile the destruction goes on. It's too fucked-up,"

"Fuckin' pigs," said the woman.

"Yeah, fuckin' pigs," said the man.

Chip's brain reeled in disbelief. His brother was a policeman. He did not like hearing them referred to as filthy barnyard animals. He felt like telling these two stupid hippies a thing or two, but remained silent. "I have to get back and study for an exam," he lied. He thanked them for their hospitality and sighed with relief as the door closed behind him. "Lousy creeps," he said to himself as he went looking for a cab to squire him back to his dormitory.

4

Joel had fooled around with several guys at the dormitory, but he found the encounters to be less than satisfying. He'd once sucked off Kenny, a tall, effeminate type, who'd fallen asleep as soon as he'd come. And overweight William, who'd sucked off Joel, wouldn't allow any kissing. "That's for faggots," he'd snorted. Joel was looking for affection and the kind of sex that went deeper than a fast orgasm.

It was about the seventh attempt that Joel had made to cruise in a gay bar. The first few times he had been too nervous when he entered. Several pairs of eyes had stripped him down as he walked through the door. He felt like a piece of meat being inspected by housewives in a supermarket, and he'd turned and left moments after arriving. He had worked up his courage, though, to the point where he made it to the bar, but he was still too self-conscious to look at anyone. One night an exceptionally good-looking young man approached him and said, "Smile. You look uptight and there's no reason to be."

"I'm not uptight," said Joel, "just mildly terrified."

After that, the conversation flowed so easily that Joel relaxed enough to feel comfortable in the unfamiliar surroundings. He knew very little about gay life and was eager to learn more. He decided he would try to seduce this stranger, just to see what would happen, but when the stranger kissed him on the lips and inserted his tongue, Joel became aroused and thought it would be best if he let the stranger seduce him. The young man invited him to go home with him, and Joel felt it was time for a formal introduction.

"By the way, my name's Joel, what's your's?"

"Michael."

"Pleased to meet you."

94

"The pleasure is all mine."

The full moon cast its glow through the naked windows of the darkened apartment. The two lay pressed against each other. While Joel savored Michael's mouth, their hands massaged each other's backs.

"You feel so good."

"So do you," whispered Michael. "Do you like getting fucked?" Joel hesitated, afraid to expose his lack of experience.

"I—I've never done it before," he finally confessed.

"Would you like to try?"

"Yes."

Michael kissed him. "If at any time, you're not into it, just let me know."

"I will."

Joel was on his back with his legs in the air. He looked up at the sculpted silhouette that hovered above, and when their eyes met, he smiled dreamily. After the lubricant had been applied—to plug and socket—Michael delicately eased himself in. When penetration was complete he whispered, "How ya doin'?"

"I never felt anything this good."

His body relaxed and his mind whirled as Michael tensed his muscles and slowly began to thrust. The strokes grew longer and more forceful, until Joel imagined a locomotive piston driving a fast-moving train. When he felt the eruption, it was electrifying and he fought tears of joy. Michael smothered him with kisses and tender words, and when his breathing became normal, suggested they change positions. Joel was amazed that Michael wanted to reciprocate. As Joel entered Michael, he thought it was too good to be true. When he came he could not believe how grand it felt. He whispered, "Did I hurt you?"

"No, it was great."

"It felt like the earth moved."

"It did."

He lay alongside Michael. They fell into a tight embrace with arms and legs all tangled up and eventually drifted into peaceful slumber. When Joel awoke the next morning, he realized that he'd finally found what he'd been looking for.

☆ ☆ ☆

In a downtown theater, Chip sat in the balcony absorbed in the incredible parade of big-breasted women who inhabited the latest film of Russ Meyer. He absently smoked a cigarette and when one unusually well-endowed actress made her ap-

95

pearance, the container of stale popcorn that had been nestled against his crotch fell to the floor between his feet, due to his uncontrollable tumescence.

☆ ☆ ☆

Jacqui sat in a corner of the Boston Public Library next to a stack of books she'd carefully selected: Adrienne Rich, Marianne Moore, Sylvia Plath, and Gwendolyn Brooks. As her eyes scanned each line, her memory tried to hold onto every word, analyzing, theorizing, juxtaposing, dissecting until her concentration wore down and she permitted her brain to cease its dizzying flight.

☆ ☆ ☆

On the roof of the boys' dormitory, Gerry and Joel were sunning themselves, in the raw, to the accompaniment of a transistor radio.

"I'm speedin' my nuts off," said Gerry. "Feels good, though."

"Feels great," said Joel.

"What are we gonna do about Dr. Walton's class?" asked Gerry.

"Good question. I've never failed anything before. I sure don't want to start now."

"Failing ain't so bad. Getting busted is worse. So's falling in love."

"I wouldn't know about that," said Joel with an exaggerated sigh. He lit a cigarette and thought about love. He had heard and used the expression all of his life, but he never really knew what it meant. Of course, he loved his parents and sister. But that wasn't the same thing as falling in love. He wondered what it was like.

☆ ☆ ☆

Martha was Medea. She was Hedda Gabler, Madame Bovary, Camille, and Anna Karenina. Sarah Bernhardt, Katherine Cornell and Bette Davis. She reached down into the depths of her soul, summoned a demon from she knew not where, and terrified her acting partner into leaping off the stage. Breathless and pale, he ran to the lavatory and threw up before he could reach the toilet.

"Very good," said her Drama coach. "But don't waste it on rehearsals. Save it for the eighth month of a run when your interest is beginning to wane."

"I'll remember," said Martha as she exited triumphantly, stage left.

Every possible flavor was available that evening at the Pewter Pot Muffin House on Boylston Street. Gerry was devouring a blueberry/corn, while Joel buttered his orange/cinnamon. With his mouth stuffed to overflowing, crumbs falling into his lap, Gerry said, "What the fuck are we gonna do about Dr. Walton's class?"

"I seem to recall you asking the same question just this afternoon."

"There's no way on earth I can do the paper, take the exam and expect to pass. I've waited too long. It's impossible."

"Same here."

They looked at each other blankly.

Gerry smiled tentatively. "We could always phone in a bomb threat."

"What?"

"A sinister plot is taking shape in my mind."

"Let's hear it," said Joel, reaching for another muffin.

"College campuses across the country are closing down because of the Kent State massacre."

"Right," said Joel, buttering a bran/currant.

"There's been a lot of pressure on the Dean to do the same here, but so far everything's status quo."

"I'm listening."

"One little ol' bomb threat would do the trick."

"You really think so?"

"Sure. One call to the Dean, one call to the police. It's too easy. And there's no danger. There won't even be a bomb. Just two phone calls."

Joel wiped his lips with a paper napkin. "Can't we be caught?"

"I don't see how. We won't be on the phone long enough for a trace, and we'll call from a booth."

"What about voice prints?"

Gerry grinned. "How many people do you know who automatically tape all their calls?"

They paid the bill and sauntered off to Kenmore Square. Walking up to a row of phone booths, Gerry said, "I'll call the Dean."

"And I'll call the cops," said Joel.

☆ ☆ ☆

Chip, Martha, and Jacqui were gathered in the Penthouse, listening to the first posthumously released recordings of Jimi

Hendrix. They were scattered about the room, in various relaxed postures, when the first buzzsaw notes of electric guitar screeched through the speakers. At first no one could differentiate between the music and the street noise, but it quickly became obvious that something was wrong. The stereo was turned down and they gathered at the windows just in time to see the police cars, firetrucks and ambulances turn the intersection below into a carnival of swirling red lights and droning sirens.

Chip ran downstairs to find out what the commotion was about, and breathlessly returned to blurt, "There's a bomb in the Student Union Building!"

"That calls for another joint," said Martha.

Just then, Joel and Gerry entered casually.

"What's up?"

"Bomb in the Student Union."

"No shit."

Joel glanced at Gerry, who looked away. At that moment they silently agreed never to reveal themselves as the culprits.

The tumult in the street below eventually subsided, and the gang turned their attention to the latest from Hendrix.

"It's kind of like robbing his grave," said Jacqui. "I mean, what if he didn't want this stuff to be released?"

"Yeah, but shit, it's here," said Gerry. "Everyone else is gonna hear it, why not us?"

"Do you think there's much more unreleased stuff?" asked Martha. "Couldn't be," replied Chip, "he was very particular and didn't record that much."

"We'll see about that," countered Joel.

When the record had been played twice, the conversation drifted back to the bomb and speculation ran high as to the consequences.

"They just might shut the campus down because of it," said Martha.

"No way," said Joel. "One bomb scare?"

Gerry stared him down and said, "Humpf!"

"In the meantime," said Chip, "let's get high. Higher than we've ever been before."

"You mean," said Gerry, "a bona-fide journey to outer space?"

"You got it."

The gang dispersed and everyone went back to their rooms to fetch their drugs. They were all reassembled in the Penthouse fifteen minutes later.

The music was loud and the smoke grew thick. There were over fifty small vials scattered everywhere containing every imaginable kind of smoking dope: hash, grass, ganja, opium, Turkish primo with streaks of white mold, and even Nepalese temple balls. Some of the vials had labels listing the contents, date purchased, and last date smoked.

It wasn't long before everyone surrendered to an attack of the munchies. Phone calls were placed and in a very short time pizzas, heroes, and Chinese food started to arrive. They stuffed themselves like it was the last meal before their execution, washed it down with cans of soda pop and once again lit up in search of that highest of highs.

They all fell asleep right where they sat, amid the overflowing ashtrays, greasy paper, sticky cartons, empty cans, pipes, papers, and roach clips.

In the morning, a mimeographed announcement was posted on every bulletin board on the college premises:

ALL CLASSES ARE SUSPENDED FOR THE REMAINDER OF THE SEMESTER. ALL STUDENTS WILL RECEIVE A 'PASS' IN ALL SUBJECTS. CLASSES WILL RESUME IN SEPTEMBER.

5

"Let me drive for a while," said Chip. He was getting restless, sitting in the back seat with no one to talk to. Joel was reading a book about the music business while Jacqui wrote a poem in a stenographer's notebook. In the front seat Martha was asleep and Gerry commanded the steering wheel.

"When I stop for gas you can drive for a while if you want to." He turned the radio up and sang along with the Stylistics' "I'm Stone In Love With You."

Martha's parents owned a house in Provincetown and apart from the summer, no one used it. A large colonial structure, it was perched right on the water near the outskirts of town. Since Gerry's parents had allowed him to take the family's second car back to Boston for second semester—and the house was empty—Martha and Gerry had planned a special weekend trip for the gang. Since school had been unexpectedly recessed and everyone hadn't planned on returning home for several weeks, a trip to Provincetown seemed like a good way to kill some time.

It was a sunny Friday afternoon, and before they went to the house, Martha wanted to stop at the market for groceries.

She directed Chip, now in the driver's seat, to the supermarket, and they all tumbled out of the car and foraged in the brightly-lit food complex. They loaded up a shopping cart with mostly junk food and got in line to pay the cashier.

Standing in front of Martha was Mark, a young man with a moustache whom she had met a couple of summers ago. When he turned and saw her there he politely inquired as to her parents' health.

"They're just great. I spoke to them on the phone a few days ago, told them I was bringing some friends down for the weekend."

"By the way, what are you doing this evening?"

"Oh, we have nothing special planned. Just gonna hang out."

"A friend of mine is having a party and he told me I could invite some people. Why don't you and your friends join us?"

Martha thanked him and accepted the small slip of paper with the address. "It's supposed to start at ten, but it probably won't get really hot until around midnight. See you later."

Martha's parents had told her that there would be a construction crew working in the backyard and that she should make her presence known to them when she arrived. When they drove up to the sprawling house there was a truck parked in the driveway, and the distant sounds of hammering and clanging hung in the briny air. After unlocking the front door and depositing the suitcases and bundles in the hall, Martha told everyone to make themselves comfortable in the living room while she went out back to talk to the men who were building the new seawall. She asked them what time they quit and invited them to come in for a beer before they left the premises. They accepted her offer and promised to knock at the back door at five o'clock.

Jacqui and Joel found the kitchen and were stocking the refrigerator when Martha returned, and subsequently took everyone upstairs to their rooms. The large house could easily accommodate them all, and the hostess insisted that they all have their own room, except for Gerry and herself, who took the master bedroom. While her guests unpacked and visited the bathrooms, Martha collected the white sheets which were draped over every item of furniture.

Eventually the gang reassembled in the living room and got down to some serious ingestion of beer, wine, and grass. The stereo played loudly, and they were all fairly stoned, so no one heard the workmen's knock which occurred punctually at five. After waiting several minutes and knocking again, the four men entered the house and followed the sound of the stereo until they found the living room.

Chip had been giving Jacqui a shotgun when the strangers hesitantly entered the large, ornate room. Taken by surprise, he became flustered and burnt his tongue with the reefer. Gerry tried to hide his stash, but it was too late. Everyone had seen. One of the men, a handsome, well-built black man stepped forward and gestured amiably, "Don't worry 'bout that stuff. We've been known to smoke it too. Sorry for the intrusion, but we were invited."

Martha stood up. "No, it's my fault. But let's forget it, okay?" Introductions were made all around, and Martha went to the kitchen to obtain four cans of cold beer. The man who had spoken appeared to be, if not the leader, then the highest in the pecking order. He introduced himself as J.T., short for Jonathan Taylor. "Everyone always called me J.T. Ever since I was a little bitty boy."

The assemblage began to relax. J.T. explained the processes involved in constructing a seawall. The gang listened attentively. Joel nudged Gerry, glanced from the stash box to the men and back to Gerry. He got the idea, but hesitated until Joel nudged him again. "Uh, you guys want to get high?"

"Love to," said J.T., "and I'm sure my friends wouldn't mind either." They nodded in assent. Gerry rolled two enormous joints, while Chip changed the record and Martha went to get more cold beer. As an afterthought, she grabbed some potato chips, pretzels and peanuts and reentered bearing a large tray. The pot-bellied man named Sam sprang to his feet and helped her. The two joints were lit simultaneously and passed around the circle in opposite directions. Sam found himself being handed both at the same time. He put them both to his lips and drew deeply, criss-crossed his arms and kept them going in their respective directions. The Lovin' Spoonful's *Greatest Hits* bounced from the speakers as the two clans drifted higher.

Sam stood up, walked over to Joel and whispered, "Where's the john?" Joel jumped to his feet and said, "Follow me."

He led him to the downstairs bathroom, adjacent to the front hall. Joel returned to the living room as the Spoonful disc was ending and replaced it with Sly and the Family Stone. When "Everyday People" came on, J.T. rose and began bumping and grinding. He danced over to Jacqui, bowed and asked her to join him. She accepted and the two were getting down in the middle of the circle when Sam returned. He walked over to the stereo, turned the volume down, spun around and shouted, "FREEZE!" In his left hand he held a badge and his right hand brandished a gun. "Here I am smokin' somethin' which is highly illegal, with a bunch of draft card and bra burners. You're all under arrest."

Gerry freaked out and bounded to his feet.

"You take one more step and you're a memory."

Gerry stood still and sheepishly put his hands in the air. Sam had an evil look in his eyes as he pointed the gun at each of them and asked, "Who'm I gonna take in? The whole bunch or just the one who owns the stuff?" Martha began to speak but Sam barked, "Shut up!"

He pointed the gun at Gerry and deliberately squeezed the trigger as Jacqui leaped to her feet and screamed, "DON'T!"

The hammer fell and made a slight, plink as Sam's evil gaze melted. He dropped the gun, laughed and slapped his thigh. "Really had ya goin', huh?"

Gerry, who had almost fainted, slowly sat down, shaking visibly.

J.T. retrieved the gun, grabbed the badge from Sam's hand and went over to Gerry. "Look, the gun's empty and the badge is a fake. Relax, kid. That's just Sam's sick sense of humor."

Sam, still laughing, went to Gerry and shook his hand. "Friends? You can take a li'l ol' joke, can't you?"

Gerry accepted the outstretched hand and shook his head in bewilderment. "Either you're a brilliant actor, or I'm one uptight motherfucker."

Martha, greatly relieved, said, "Or perhaps a little of both."

With everybody back at ease, Martha said, "Hey, Gerry, roll another one, just like the other one." The music was turned up and the room became enveloped in a smoky haze. J.T. looked at his watch and announced that he had to go. Sam interjected, "Ya got another hot date?"

"That's right."

"Ol' J.T. here always has a date on Friday night, ain't that right? And you know what? She must be uglier than hell or more beautiful than Miss America, 'cause none of us has ever seen 'er."

"I don't kiss and tell," said J.T.

"Maybe she's married."

"Drop it, Sam." He thanked Gerry for the grass and Martha for her hospitality. The two shy men who had not said a word until they said goodbye, and Sam shook hands all around. They left the house, got in the truck and were soon out of sight. Joel and Jacqui went around the room collecting empties and dumping ashtrays while Martha prepared an enormous pot of spaghetti and tomato sauce which yielded portions that were big enough to leave everyone feeling that they had eaten too much. Afterwards they went for a stroll along the dunes.

☆ ☆ ☆

It was approximately eleven-thirty when the gang arrived at the address which Martha had obtained at the supermarket earlier that day. She rang the buzzer and a tall, slim man wearing a sailor suit and cap opened the door.

"Good evening. Please come in and leave your inhibitions behind you." He bowed grandly and stepped aside as the gang entered and huddled by the door. Martha explained that Mark Thompson had extended the invitation and introduced her friends.

"Pleased to meet you all. Just call me Mary. I'm known far and wide as Provincetown Mary." He smiled broadly and continued as he led them into the parlor. "Mark said he might not make it 'til late because he and Bill might fuck more than usual. If you can imagine that."

Mary showed them to the bar and told them to help themselves. Eyeing Chip up and down, he said, "You're kind of cute."

Chip blushed and looked away.

"Let me introduce you around."

There were two boys on the couch, both dressed identically in LaCoste shirts, black Levi's and Topsiders. Their names were Jeff and Tony and they were both strikingly handsome. Sitting next to them were a well-muscled man and a heavy, short-haired woman. The man, Arnold, had an effeminate inflection in his speech and his eyes lit up when he was introduced to Joel. The woman, Phoebe, spoke with evenly measured tones and politely said hello to everyone. There were two women dressed in jeans and sweatshirts holding hands near the stereo and a very elegantly-dressed, emaciated man named Paul who replaced Smokey Robinson and the miracles with the Broadway Cast album of *Company*. Mary moved around the room clearing away empty glasses, refilling the candy dish and fetching fresh drinks.

103

Gerry extracted a few joints from his cigarette pack and passed them around. Martha had started talking to Paul about Stephen Sondheim, while Joel and Jacqui joined Arnold and Phoebe in a discussion about oppressed minorities. Chip and Gerry stood near the bar. "Can you believe this?" said Chip.

"Too much. Every time I think I've seen it all, BOOM. This could prove to be very interesting. 'Nother cocktail?"

"You bet."

Martha followed Mary into the kitchen. "Can I try on your sailor cap, please?"

"Of course, darling. Let me help. Oooo, it really suits you." The doorbell rang, and while Mary went to answer it, Martha reappeared in the parlor, twirling the sailor cap on the extended pointer of her right hand.

When Mary returned with the newly arrived guests, Joel was the first to notice that one of the two men standing in the doorway was J.T., leader of the construction crew. Stepping over to Joel, J.T. shook his hand and said, "I'd like you to meet Stuart, my lover. Stuart, this is Joel."

They shook hands. "Pleased to meet you," said Stuart.

J.T. moved around the room shaking hands with everyone, except for tuxedoed Paul, whom he hugged and kissed. Mary, who was standing next to Chip and Gerry at the bar whispered, "Paul and J.T. were lovers until Stuart stepped into the picture. But they're all friends now."

"Oh, really," said Chip.

Martha was stunned because she did not think that a person could be a construction worker and gay, but she did her best to appear unperturbed. She tried to find traces of effeminate behavior in his actions, but he was the same masculine guy he had appeared to be before. She figured that J.T. must be the "butch" and Stuart the "femme," but she was unable to detect any feminine mannerisms in Stuart either.

Arnold had gone to the bathroom and Phoebe was giving Jacqui the eye. Embarrassed, Joel went over to the bar.

"Is there anything I can get for you," asked Mary.

"Well, actually," said Joel, "is there anyone here who could sell me a hit of speed?"

"Hmmm. Let me think. I don't speed anymore myself. Bad for the skin. Wait a minute. Fred and Robert. They should be here soon. They always do speed. I'm sure you can get some from them. I'll talk to them as soon as they get here."

"Thanks. It's a terrific party and I want to keep my energy level up."

"You know, a girl could kind of go for you."

Mary placed his hand on Joel's shoulder. Joel became nervous with this queen in sailor drag touching him in front of his friends, but he did not want his uneasiness to show. He forced a smile and said, "You're not exactly my type."

Mary feigned indignation and said, "That's the story of my life." He sashayed away in an exaggerated huff.

Chip and Arnold discussed body-building techniques, while Martha and Gerry chatted about theater, film and acting with the look-alikes Jeff and Tony, who it turned out, were lovers and had dramatic aspirations themselves. Mary fussed in the kitchen and replenished ice, canapes, and M&Ms.

Mark Thompson finally arrived with his boyfriend, a burly man of indeterminate age. They mixed drinks for themselves and circled the room, greeting their friends. Jacqui, Phoebe and J.T. sat on the floor in front of the large speakers and sang along with the Rolling Stones' *High Tide and Green Grass*, while J.T.'s current lover, Stuart, danced with his ex-lover, Paul.

The doorbell rang and when Mary answered it to find Fred and Robert, he remembered that Joel had inquired about some speed. He explained the situation to them. Mary ushered them in and after they greeted their friends, introduced them to Joel.

Joel's eyes widened. Fred, though not very handsome, was very sexy. In skintight white Levi's the tapered columns of his thighs and the bulge of his crotch made Joel weak with desire. Robert was as cute as the underwear models in the back of *Playboy*. He smiled at Joel. "If you like, you can come over to our place. It's only a five minute walk and we've got plenty of black beauties."

"You're sure it wouldn't be any trouble?"

"Actually, it would be a pleasure. Besides, we'll be back in no time." Joel explained the situation to Martha and left with the two young men. Paul drew Mary aside and asked, "When are you going to do your Judy Garland number?"

"Give me a few minutes to change."

"I'll change the record after a few more songs."

An entire wall of Mary's apartment was decorated with posters of Broadway musicals, and Martha and Gerry were looking at them, listing the ones they'd both seen. Meanwhile, the two women in jeans and sweatshirts were slow dancing cheek to cheek. They accidentally bumped into the TV tray which supported the potato chips and California onion dip and it went crashing to the floor with debris scattering in all directions. Mary couldn't hear the commotion with his bedroom door closed and thought it was time for his entrance. He bounded into the parlor in complete Judy Garland drag and stepped into a large mound of onion dip. He slipped and fell, spattering the red gown, pumps and wig with stains that he was never able to remove. He sighed, got to his feet, and went back to the bedroom to change. Jacqui cleaned up the mess and Mary returned wearing the familiar sailor suit.

☆ ☆ ☆

When Joel entered Fred and Robert's apartment he was struck by the beauty and sophistication of the decor. The vases of flowers, paintings in gilded frames and uniform leatherbound volumes made a tremendous impression. Robert asked if he'd like to sit and offered him a drink.

"Are you going to have one?" asked Joel.

"Yes."

"I'll have whatever you're getting for yourself."

"Rum and coke?"

"Fine."

Fred, meanwhile, returned from the bedroom with a joint and a vial of pills. "Smoke?"

"Sure," said Joel, "Why not?"

The three of them sat on the sofa, with Joel in the middle, and when the joint was finished, Robert picked up the vial and handed it to him. "Help yourself," he said as he patted Joel's thigh. He opened the vial, took out one capsule, placed it on his tongue and washed it down with a swig of his cocktail. Fred had his arm on the back of the sofa behind Joel's head and he eased it down so that it cradled Joel's shoulders. Joel glanced down at Fred's crotch.

"Would you like to hear some music?" asked Fred.

"Sure."

Fred mussed Joel's hair, stood up and played "The First Time Ever I Saw Your Face" by Roberta Flack. Robert had shifted his leg so that it was leaning against Joel's and the tentative touching of his thigh had graduated to a regular stroke. Joel became nervous, gulped his drink and glanced at Robert. When their eyes met, Joel shuddered. He felt a sinking sensation in his stomach. Robert took his hand. His palms became

106

sweaty and he blushed with embarrassment. Fred sat down and dropped his arm around Joel's shoulders.

"So, Joel, what are you into?" purred Robert.

"Well," said Joel, clearing his throat, "I write and sing and would someday like to make records and give concerts. But right now I'm majoring in English Literature."

"That's wonderful. Do you like Jane Austen?"

"I haven't read her yet."

"You should read *Pride and Prejudice* and *Mansfield Park*. They're both excellent." The three sat and listened to the music. Fred played with Joel's hair and Robert held his hand. Beginning to relax, Joel suddenly felt his cock begin to stir. He hoped that they wouldn't notice, but it felt too good to suppress. He turned to Fred and asked, "What are you thinking about?"

Fred smiled. "Kissing you."

Staring into his eyes, Fred touched his cheek and slowly brought his head forward until their lips met. Planting his mouth firmly over Joel's, he gently drew Joel's tongue into his mouth and sucked it as though it were something precious and rare. Joel felt himself growing more erect as his body began to tingle all over. He slowly pulled away and was still looking into Fred's eyes when he felt Robert's grip on his hand tighten.

"It's my turn," said Robert as he turned Joel's face to his. The deep, lapis lazuli eyes riveted his gaze as he received Robert's eager tongue. Robert explored Joel's mouth as Fred's hand closed over his stiff cock, straining against the faded denim. Joel began to breathe faster. He allowed his body to roll with the flow. Seconds later, his warm fluid sprang forth and collected on the fabric of his snug, white briefs.

☆ ☆ ☆

When the three returned to the party at Mary's, several guests had already gone. Those remaining were all offered capsules from the tiny vial. Everybody took one. They all sat in a circle on the floor, smoking, drinking, and speed rapping until dawn, while the same Santana album played over and over.

6

The gang splintered into five individuals for the summer break and regrouped at the beginning of September. Martha, Gerry and Joel worked as a waitress, cab driver and summer camp counselor, respectively. Jacqui taught reading and writing for a Head Start program and Chip tooled around Indiana in his new MG.

Living arrangements for the third semester were slightly different from the previous year. Joel and Chip rented a small railroad flat on Marlborough Street. Martha and Gerry moved into a tiny studio on the same block, a few buildings away. Jacqui was back at her dormitory, this time with a room to herself.

Thunderous applause greeted Jacqui as she stepped down from the podium. The reading, her second, had gone exceedingly well. The audience loved her. She was deluged with compliments and thanks from the largely female, mostly feminist crowd. Among her admirers was a statuesque black woman who moved with antelope grace. With beribboned braided hair and warm, brown eyes, her name was Elaine and she had cried when Jacqui read her epic verse, "Hecate's Clock."

After the throng had dissipated somewhat, Elaine approached Jacqui. She took her hands, locked her gaze on Jacqui's eyes and profusely thanked the poetess for sharing her sensitivity and insight. Jacqui was too overwhelmed to say anything. When Elaine finally broke the silence, Jacqui accepted her invitation. They walked to Elaine's small, but nicely furnished apartment. African ceremonial masks decorated the walls, and wicker chairs were grouped around a circular, mahogany coffee table.

Sipping brandy, they listened to Sarah Vaughn and Nina Simone. They talked about poetry, the women's movement and bebop. Elaine finally admitted that she wrote poetry and Jacqui insisted on reading some.

"Not now. I can loan them to you. Read them when I'm not around." They moved closer. And found themselves touching each other to emphasize their thoughts and words. They kissed and when Elaine asked if she would care to spend the night, Jacqui was enthralled.

The two lithe forms lay together on the bed. They whispered silly things to each other. "Chocolate Lover." "Ebony Princess." They kissed and hugged and played with each other's breasts. Their breathing became deeper, their passions merged. They satisfied each other with their mouths, every so often substituting their fingers while they rested their tongues. When each was completely spent, they tried to sleep, but were far too excited. They talked and touched, hugged and kissed, until the first motes of sunlight danced over the windowsill.

☆ ☆ ☆

Martha, Jacqui, and Joel were sitting in a tiny movie theater on Boylston Street when Gerry rushed over to them and breathlessly asked, "How much time 'til it starts?"

"A few minutes. You still have time to get some popcorn," said Joel. "What's the name of this film again?"

"*The Seventh Seal*," said Jacqui.

"Fellini or Truffaut?"

"Bergman," said Martha.

"Oh. Where's Chip?"

"He only goes to movies that have dumb broads with big tits," chuckled Joel.

☆ ☆ ☆

The old television set that Gerry's parents had given him was broken again, and he was scribbling in his notebook. Martha wanted to watch *Casablanca*, so she called to see if Joel or Chip was at home and if their television was available. Joel answered and told her to come over.

Martha, Joel, and Chip sat in the living room sipping beer, while Humphrey Bogart and Ingrid Bergman inhabited the small screen. About halfway through the film, Joel yawned, stretched and went to his room. Martha and Chip watched the entire film. As the credits were rolling by, Martha donned her jacket.

"Don't leave yet," said Chip. "Stay and smoke a joint with me."

"Okay."

He turned off the television and they quietly entered Chip's room. He closed the door.

They passed a Jamaican joint laced with Panama red back and forth, sitting next to one another on the mattress on the floor. Emboldened by the fragrant smoke, Chip began to flirt. "I hope Gerry knows what a helluva woman you are." He stroked her long, dark hair. "Such soft hair. I'll bet he's about the luckiest guy in the universe."

"Come off it ya big lug. You wouldn't even give me the time of day. My tits are too small."

They laughed.

"I wish I could develop my breasts the way you've developed your arms. I like a man with all his bulges in the right places." She winked.

"If you think my arms are good, you should see my calves."

Martha shuddered. "Well," she said, "are you gonna show me?"

109

"Let's make a deal. Do you want the box or what's behind the curtain. But seriously, folks, if you take off your blouse, I'll take off my pants."

"Sounds fair."

Chip stood up and unzipped his jeans. Martha unbuttoned her shirt. He sat down. They studied each other for a minute and then kissed. He pulled her down and licked her nipples. The remaining clothing was removed. They embraced and flew into a frenzy of wet kisses, their bodies writhing around on the mattress. The attraction was strong, but neither could completely erase the thoughts of Gerry that kept returning to interfere. Chip and Martha fooled around all night long, but neither achieved the heights of sensuality and release of which they were usually so capable.

The next morning, they awoke and could barely look at one another. They spoke a few awkward words. Martha tried to leave discretely. But Joel emerged from his room just as she was leaving Chip's room. Immediately grasping the situation, Joel frowned. He glared at them as they stood by the door, Martha's usually perfect hair, dishevelled, and Chip in his briefs. Martha tried to explain, but Joel interrupted. "Don't tell me anything. I don't want to know."

Chip entreated him to let him explain, but he grew angrier. He moved toward the front door, trying to suppress his rage, when Martha blurted, "Please don't tell Gerry."

"He'll never hear about it from me," snapped Joel, "I can guarantee you that!"

When he slammed the door behind him, the small glass hash pipe that Joel kept on his shelf, fell to the floor and shattered.

☆ ☆ ☆

Gerry had never been much of a reader, except, for magazine articles about his favorite blues singers and rock stars. One day he stopped by a bookstore to pick up a copy of *The Rimers Of Eldritch* by Lanford Wilson for Martha. He was very high and found himself wandering around the stacks, looking at the illustrations on the covers of paperbacks, when he stumbled upon *Confessions Of An English Opium Eater* by Thomas DeQuincey. It had never occurred to him that there might exist a body of literature on the subject of transcendental drugs. He bought it, devoured it and was hungry for more. He subsequently discovered *Artificial Paradise* by Charles Baudelaire, *The Doors Of Perception* by Aldous Huxley, *M'Hashish* by Mo-

110

hammed Mrabet, *A Separate Reality* by Carlos Castaneda and *The Yage Letters* by Allen Ginsberg and William S. Burroughs. Gerry became a lover of books, seemingly overnight, and began to haunt the cluster of tiny book stores that pepper the streets around Harvard Square, in search of any and all material that pertained to his newly-discovered literary genre.

7

Bring 'em home, bring 'em home.
Stop the war and bring 'em home.
Thousands of people had gathered in the Common to protest the continuation of the war, and the gang, plus Elaine, all stood beneath the Black Lesbians For Peace banner. The park was packed with flower children, militant students, and the National Guard.

Jacqui had convinced the gang that they should all march together and decided it would be the perfect opportunity to introduce Elaine to her friends. When the march had ended and the rally began, Elaine unpacked her picnic hamper and passed around alfalfa sprout sandwiches and thermoses of apple cider.

"This is great," said Chip, maneuvering a few stray sprouts into his mouth. "I'm glad you like them," Elaine smiled and her perfect white teeth sparkled. "Try some of this," she said, handing him a thermos. He swigged freely.

"Wow, this is hard stuff."

Elaine giggled and passed the thermos to Martha. Jacqui took Elaine's hand and kissed it.

"That's so sweet," said Gerry, raising Martha's hand to his lips. The speaker, a well-known civil rights leader, droned away in the background. Joel strained to hear the words but they were inaudible.

"Elaine has asked me to move in with her," said Jacqui.

"No kidding," said Joel.

Martha swallowed. "And you accepted, I hope."

Jacqui and Elaine beamed at her and nodded their heads.

"When's the big day?" asked Gerry.

"Soon," said Jacqui, "very soon."

"Can I have another sandwich?" asked Chip.

"Of course," said Elaine, reaching for one.

"Swig o' cider," said Gerry, taking the thermos from Martha.

Just then, a skinny dude in patched jeans came by hawking Peace & Love t-shirts. Gerry bought six and handed them out to the picnicking peaceniks. He ripped off his plain t-shirt and donned the new one. Jumping to his feet, he started chanting. *Peace now, peace now*, punctuating the air with his fist. The gang leaped to their feet and joined him. Soon everyone nearby did the same and eventually the chant was seized by everyone gathered in the park.

☆ ☆ ☆

Joel stepped off the tiny stage to the accompaniment of scattered, but enthusiastic applause. Carefully placing his guitar in the plush-lined, hard-shell case, he sat down and ordered a coke when the waitress came by. He had been spending more time with his guitar, perfecting his picking style, developing his voice and composing folky pop songs. Finally working up the courage, he had come to the Sword In The Stone on Charles Street to try out his new material. He was pleased with his performance and satisfied by the audience's response. He lit a cigarette when his drink arrived and wondered if he should approach the club owner for a booking. His thoughts were interrupted when a stranger came over to his table and addressed him in a quiet voice.

"You're really good. I loved your stuff. Especially the last song. Did you write it?"

"Yes. I wrote 'em all."

"That's amazing . . .would you mind if I sat down for a minute?"

Joel took in the sensitive green eyes, thick waves of brown hair, and pouting mouth. He gestured at the empty chair. The stranger ordered a Seven-Up and the two fell into animated conversation that centered on Tim Hardin, Tom Paxton and Phil Ochs. Feeling that the stranger's eyes were trying to probe his innermost thoughts, Joel looked down at the table, trying to avoid the intense gaze. The stranger lit a cigarette and inhaled deeply. "Have you ever heard of Bruce Mackay? He has an album out on ESP?"

"I don't think so," replied Joel.

"I live right around the corner, and I thought you might like to come over and listen to it."

Joel pondered the suggestion for a few seconds, then explained that he would gladly go over, but first he wanted to talk business with the club owner. When he returned to the table he found that the bill for the two sodas had been paid.

"Thank you."

"Well, are you gonna work here, or what?"

"The guy said he was busy when I was on, but he noticed that the audience's response was positive, so he told me to come back next week and he'd give me a solid listen."

"Do you believe him?"

"Do I have a choice?"

They sat on the couch in the stranger's shabby apartment, listening to the Bruce Mackay record. Joel was enjoying it and began to relax when the stranger abruptly turned to him and introduced himself, apologizing for not having done so before. "The name's Zack."

"Joel."

"Yeah, I know, they introduced you at the club, remember?" Zack ran his finger along Joel's cheekbone and kissed him. Joel buried his hands in Zack's thick hair as they scoured the insides of each other's mouths. Gripped in a bear-hug embrace, they rolled around on the couch. Stripping themselves, they lay down alongside one another on the couch. Zack propped some throw pillows against the armrest. As Zack nibbled his earlobe and played with his cock, Joel closed his eyes and pictured Chip.

☆ ☆ ☆

The Drama Department's production of *Hamlet* opened a few weeks before the end of the third semester and Martha's Ophelia was dazzling. The college paper's theater critic singled out her performance as the strongest. The gang sat together on opening night. Joel and Chip threw a party at their apartment afterwards, and Martha was buzzing with excitement.

"You're going to be a great actress," said Chip.

"You're already a great actress," said Elaine.

"Here, here," said Jacqui, raising her glass in tribute.

"You were sensational," said Joel.

"Thank you," said Martha.

"I love you," said Gerry, kissing her cheek.

Martha sipped her champagne and smiled at Chip. He grinned, toasted her, then looked away.

☆ ☆ ☆

Jacqui was the first to drop out of school. Elaine had encouraged her to send a sheaf of poems to a small publisher and when she received the notice of acceptance, she decided to quit and start writing full time. She moved into Elaine's apartment on St. Botolph Street. *Circle Of Stars*, her collected poems, was published six months later. It was dedicated to "The Gang Of Five."

☆ ☆ ☆

Martha and Gerry's studio, usually saturated with loud music, and thick smoke had become very quiet and sober. A layer of dust had settled over Gerry's record collection. Most evenings, Gerry lay on his stomach on the bed reading, and Martha sat in the easy chair memorizing lines.

One night she put down the script, walked to the bed and pounced. "Not now," he said and rolled away.

She tickled him.

"Quit."

She moved away from the bed and brushed her hair.

"I'm sorry, it's just that I'm obsessed with this stuff," he said, slapping the book with his palm.

"I know," she sighed.

"I have an idea," he said, sitting up. He crossed his legs and pushed his hair from his forehead.

"Oh, what's that?"

"I'm gonna make a film."

"Really," she said haughtily, "can I play the femme fatale?"

"A documentary. About famous writers who wrote about drugs."

"That sounds interesting. I've been thinking about a few ideas myself." She put the brush down on the dresser.

"Like what?"

"Like finding a school with a better drama department."

"What's wrong with the one you've got?"

"It's always classics. We never do anything modern."

Gerry lit a joint and offered it to her, but she waved it away. "I've been checking out some catalogs and I'm thinking about applying to the Academy of Dramatic Arts."

"That's in New York?"

"Right."

"Funny," he said, "I've been thinking about moving back there to try and raise some money for my film."

☆ ☆ ☆

It was a cold, blustery day, the wind slipping through the chinks in Joel and Chip's apartment. Joel had just returned from an audition at a folk club and Chip was sitting in a tattered armchair, listening to Led Zeppelin. Joel turned the stereo down.

114

"We have to talk."

"Shoot."

"Well, I've been thinking about it a lot and I decided I don't want to study English Lit anymore. I'm going to apply to a music school and learn piano and composition. You can find another roommate or keep the place by yourself, but I'll be out by next semester."

Chip lit a joint and passed it to Joel. "Strange you should bring it up, ol' buddy, but I think I'm gonna go too."

Joel inhaled and handed the joint back. Chip sucked in a large toke and said, "With Martha and Gerry in New York and Jacqui writing all the time, it's not as much fun as it used to be. Besides, I feel like forgetting all this bullshit and going back home. There's a good job waiting for me at my father's radio station."

The night before Chip was to return to Indiana, he invited Joel to join him for dinner at The Crossroads.

A modest place with red and white checkered tablecloths and Chianti bottle candle holders, the restaurant featured a large menu of Italian dishes. Chip and Joel ate garlic bread and sipped red wine while they waited for their lasagna.

"I'm gonna miss you, buddy. The others too. But I guess it's time to get serious. Settle down to a good job. Get married. The whole damn thing."

"I know what you mean. I've had a good time, learned a few things about myself," he hesitated for a moment, "and now I know what I really want to do. Be a professional musician. And Jacqui getting her book published made me realize that the longer I put it off, the longer it's gonna take."

They ate in silence and finished off the bottle of wine. Chip bought another on the way back to the apartment and uncorked it as soon as they were inside.

"Vino?"

Joel put his hands to his head. "I think I've had enough."

"Not me."

They sat and watched television until Joel noticed that Chip was snoring. He turned off the TV and tried to rouse Chip. He was unreachable. Joel struggled to get Chip to his feet and dragged him, stumbling with the weight, to bed. Joel looked down at the body sprawled on the bed. He unbuttoned Chip's faded work shirt and lifted his torso to get the arms through the sleeves. Unzipping the jeans, he peeled them from Chip's muscular legs. The jockey shorts and sweat socks were easier to remove. He looked at Chip's perfect body, wished that he could lay down alongside and hold it tight, but silently said goodbye and brought the blanket to Chip's throat.

The next afternoon, Joel helped Chip carry his luggage to the waiting taxi. They embraced on the sidewalk and promised to stay in touch. Joel watched the car disappear into the traffic and went back inside. He unpacked his guitar and strummed an e minor chord until the sun had gone down and the moonlight had transformed the room into shadows.

T.N.Y.C.G.M.F.W.*

"You know, Mort, I've said it before, it's really not a good idea to write about writers." Lighting a cigarette, the man with orange hair glared at his victim. "People don't like to read about writers. They're interested in characters with *real* jobs."

The older man blanched, cleared his throat and shot back, "What makes you think that being a lawyer is more interesting than being a journalist?" He nervously looked around the room.

"Hey, now Mort, calm down. I'm not attacking your profession, just this ridiculous story . . ."

"Excuse me for interrupting, Red," said James, the slim young man who sat next to Mort on the sofa, "but according to Beckett, in his famous book on Proust . . ."

"Proust again?" said Daniel, playing with the left shoulder strap of his white tank top. "Who the fuck is this Proust, anyway? I thought we were talkin' 'bout Mort's short story . . ."

"Proust," snarled James, "happened to have been one of the great . . ."

"Wait a minute," said Red. He paused dramatically and sipped from his coffee mug. "Before we get into a long digression about that pedantic French bore, let's get back to Mort's story. Okay?"

Mort looked down at his manuscript while Daniel forsook his shoulder strap to scratch his crotch. James shot a disapproving look at Red and snapped, "God'll get you for failing to appreciate the foremost non-living litterateur of the Twentieth Century . . . now, about Mort's story . . . I think the charac-

* The New York City Gay Men's Fiction Workshop

ters, plot and tone are all fine, but the description is too sketchy. Now take Proust, for example. He could describe the leaf of a tree in several thousand different ways."

"James, darling," said Mort, "I'm not trying to write like Proust. I'm more of a Hemingway nut myself and . . ."

"*Hemingway!* Barf-O!" chuckled Red as he put his finger down his throat. He stood up and stretched. "I think it's time for a break. More coffee, anyone?"

"Thanks," said James, "just a half a cup this time."

"I gotta pee," said Daniel. His springy body uncoiled and glided into the hall as Mort fingered his toupee to insure its position.

"Mort?"

"No more for me, dear, how about some water?"

"Coming right up." The red-headed hulk sashayed into the kitchen as Mort's gaze settled onto James' boyish face.

"So, how are things going at the book store?"

"Terrific," sighed James. "I just got a raise."

"That's nice . . . my interview with Dustin Hoffman was just published in *Film Comment.*"

James offered a phony yawn.

"You're looking very well these days, James. It gladdens the heart of an older man just to look at young, attractive males."

Ignoring the compliment, James looked away. Daniel entered the living room and strode to the bar. He poured himself a shot of Black Label and lowered his body into the paisley easy chair. Just then, Red returned bearing a circular tray, his damp t-shirt clinging to his overly developed torso. "It's getting hot in here. Think I'll close the window and turn on the air conditioner."

"*Fabulous* idea," chimed Mort.

The telephone rang and Red charged into the bedroom to answer it. Daniel burped and stared straight at James' face as though it were a target. "Strange runnin' into *you* at the Saint!"

"I go there from time to time," said James.

"I didn't think that high-brow lit'rary types had time for somethin' like dancin'."

"Who goes to dance? I like the parade."

"I saw you talkin' to Scott Calisher . . . y'know he usta be *mine.*"

James wound his index finger into the bronze curlicue that

dangled over his left ear. "Don't you think it would be far more accurate to say that you were *his*?"

Daniel took a sip of scotch. "We're discussin' the first chapter of your novel next week?"

"Yes," James nodded.

"Good," grinned Daniel.

Red jogged into the living room. "Sorry, gents, but it was a rather *pressing* call."

"Oh?" said Mort. "Did your boyfriend's gerbil crawl under the refrigerator again?"

Red laughed. "No, actually, my sister's getting married next month and . . ."

"Look," Daniel interrupted, "I don't give a flyin' fuck about your sister's sex life and I gotta split by ten."

"Can we get back to my story now?" pleaded Mort. "All these interruptions . . . I lose track."

"If I'm not mistaken," said James, "it's Daniel's turn to share his lit'rary expertise."

Daniel lit a cigarette and glared at Mort. "How d'ya 'spect me to finish a story with no int'restin' characters or plot? I got to page seven and nothin' happened, so I quit."

"What do you mean, *nothing happened*. In the first paragraph the narrator receives a telegram from his brother who has been presumed dead . . ."

"What Daniel meant," interjected James, "is that there were no hot studs or steamy sex scenes, therefore his attention was not sufficiently engaged. Is that correct?" He looked at Daniel and faked a yawn.

"Yeah, somethin' like that."

"I think what Daniel is trying to say," said Red, "is that your story does not contain any characters or turns of plot to which he can relate."

"But I didn't write this story for illiterate disco bunnies. It's supposed to be a tender look at what it means to grow old as a gay person combined with a suspense angle . . ."

"Yes, Mort, we figured that out," said James, exasperated. "Your writing lacks solid exposition. You need to describe things more metaphorically and . . ."

The doorbell rang, surprising everyone. Friends were told to stay away when a writer's group meeting was in progress.

"Excuse me!" Red bounded to the hall and stalked to the door. Shushing Clifford, he guided him to the bedroom and closed the door. He fetched a wad of bills and traded it for a glassine envelope. Dipping into the alabaster powder with his long pinky nail, he fed each of the four nostrils present, which flared eagerly like the beaks of newly born birds at feeding time. Shushing Clifford again, he led him to the door and closed it behind him. He returned to his guests. "Sorry for the interruption but the Super had to check out my fire escape. Now, where were we?"

Red looked at Mort.

Mort looked at James.

James looked bored.

Daniel looked at his wristwatch. "I gotta go . . . we can meet at my place next time."

The others froze. Simply walking down Daniel's block was like confronting a construction crew with the possibility that they might be something less than Real Men. Daniel rose and Mort whined, "But we're not through with my story!"

"Look," said Red, "who wants to read a story with a cliched inheritance scam involving an old, gay man? A *writer* yet!"

The Crystal Storm

Sitting on the sofa, upholstered with the dyed pelts of native beasts, Mahr gazed out the window and wept. His long hair, the color of mother-of-pearl with highlights of pink, gray, and blue, ran in rivulets down his neck. They tumbled across tanned shoulders that were too broad and powerful to belong to anyone but a Warrior King. A gauze tunic with narrow shoulder straps loosely hiding the hard torso was cinched at the waist with a gold chain. It hung to mid-thigh, concealing the iron codpiece that protected the ruler.

A large wooden door opposite the sofa creaked open and Sergon, the ruler's godfather, slowly entered the chamber. A domesticated beast raised itself in the corner and growled menacingly, the black fur around its snout bristling with fury.

"Silence, Shogar! Sit!" Mahr's voice, weak and weary, displayed none of the power for which it had become known. But the beast relaxed and rested its head on its paws.

"And how is my master this evening?" asked Sergon, his voice cracked and reedy.

Mahr, blinking away a tear, looked at him and replied, "Nothing has changed. The crystals look particularly threatening tonight. I am lonely. That is all."

Sergon rubbed his bald scalp with his upper right hand, an unconscious gesture that indicated concern. "Is there nothing I can do?"

Mahr looked away and watched the crystals exploding against the windowpane.

"Will my master not eat this evening?"

Mahr offered no reply.

"If my master needs mo, surely he will ring." Sergon left the study and returned to his suite.

The crystals — tiny symmetrical shards of ice — shattered against the stone walls and glass windows of the fortress of Mahr. Long were the shadows on the surrounding gardens, cast from the stars and moons that glimmered in the dark sky. Gale winds sent the glinting crystals, some tinged cerulean, some scarlet, swirling around the naked trees and shrubs. They danced in the lights from the sky until collision with any solid object caused them to shatter in kaleidoscopic explosions. And the winds were unusually fierce that evening, despite their artificial origin. The dancing fireworks made auras around the trees, shrubs, and walls that encircle the fortress, itself the target of a million shimmering crystals.

Within the fortress were many chambers; some barren, some practical, and others ostentatious with finery and technology. One such room, the ruler's study, was lit from within by hundreds of candles, each in its own sconce, situated variously about the walls. A large screen, studded with many colored light bulbs, hung on the wall adjacent to the sofa, the lights flickering in an unvarying pattern. A light show that signalled no danger from predatory enemies, no chinks in the defense mechanism of Mahr's regime. A strange primitive style of Earth music — inverted clam shell marimbas, bowed catgut strings and conch trumpets — filled the study with primordial song.

Mahr lowered the volume of the elaborate sound system and walked to the bookcase, his calf muscles clenching like fists, and selected a large leather-bound tome. *Tales Of Bold Comrades In Combat, In Love* by Landragon. A standard text of the warrior class, lyric prose poems of homoerotic love. Mahr sat and began reading the words which had taken him away so many times before. Away from the pressure of owning land, ruling a planet, leading a race, fighting a cold war. Away also from the loneliness that comes with too few opportunities to meet suitable love partners. When Mahr was younger and still in training, there were always sturdy lads with whom he could gambol, wrestle, lock loins. But having risen to responsibility, his time was spent serving his transplanted tribe. The precious leisure time lost to staying in shape, reading reports and plotting strategies.

Mahr's eyes, clearer now that the tears had stopped, plunged into the story of Drango and Vixley — a heroic sea captain and his cabin boy. The legend says that it was only Drango's unyielding love for the handsome boy that gave him the strength and will to defeat the invading armada. As Mahr approached his favorite part of the tale—the description of the two disrobing—his reading was suddenly interrupted by the tolling of the visitor's bell which echoed through the corridors of the fortress. Confident that Sergon or another of his retinue would admit the guest, repel the insurgents or give direction to one who'd lost his way, Mahr resumed reading. A few moments later, Sergon entered the chamber and Mahr closed the book with a sigh.

"Master, you have a visitor. He is unknown to me, but the weapon detector and brain scan reveal that he is unarmed and most definitely not hostile."

"Find out what he wants and report back."

"You might want to interrogate this one yourself. It is long since one as handsome as he has crossed the threshold of this place."

Mahr returned the book to its shelf. "Summon the stranger. Prepare some food and drink."

The techno-winds changed direction and the clinking of the crystals on the window ceased. Mahr reached for the cylindrical scepter that rested in a contoured box lined with green velvet. He turned it over in his hand and studied the bizarre hieroglyphics etched into the ceramic heirloom. "Oh, scepter of my family's power, symbol of all that is good and evil, focus me. Mother of nature, Father of time, help me to find peace for my people, solace for myself."

He returned the dream wand to its case and wiped the sweat from his forehead. Just then, the massive door creaked open and the stranger entered the candle-lit chamber.

"Welcome," said Mahr.

"Thank you," replied the stranger. His fine features and dark, brown skin formed the perfect setting for the black eyes that shone like polished ebony. His thick, curlicued hair cascaded over the white headband that circled his forehead and could be glimpsed intermittently all around his delicately shaped skull. Mahr took note of the tight-fitting trousers and shirt cut from a metallic fabric, the raiment of a scholar. "My name is Vraylok. I am humbled to meet Mahr, whose deeds are known throughout the galaxy."

"Won't you sit? This sofa is most comfortable." Vraylok stepped around the table before the sofa and lowered himself. "You are humanoid," said Mahr. "Much like myself except for the coloring."

123

"Yes, we are both descended from Earth refugees."

"You know of Earth?" asked Mahr incredulously.

"Yes. I know the history of the Earthlings, for it is my ancestors' history as well."

"My godfather is preparing nourishment. Say that you will share our bounty."

"I accept your generous hospitality and will someday reciprocate."

"That is not necessary," said Mahr as he increased the volume of the music. "It is my pleasure to offer you the comforts of my home. I have food and liqueurs, game rooms, sights and sounds for amusement, a library for research. Stay as long as you like. Sir, you are most welcome."

Vraylok looked about the cavernous room, glanced at the growling beast in the corner, the shifting pattern on the defense screen. Mahr looked at his guest, the sinewy musculature and intelligent eyes, trying to suppress the sensation of lust that was spreading throughout his body. The codpiece suddenly felt too tight and confining.

Sergon reappeared and placed a large tray on the table. With his two left hands he deftly maneuvered food and utensils before the guest. With his right hands he performed — with perfect symmetry — the same preparations for his master. Bowing, he retreated silently. Vraylok was amazed at the display of manual dexterity.

"This man you call 'godfather', what are his origins?"

"He is humanoid, like ourselves. But descended from a mutant strain which developed from overexposure to radiation. Through selective breeding and genetic alteration, a race was created that has full use of four upper body limbs. Sergon is, like myself, the last of his family. He has looked after me since my birth. A more devoted ally would be difficult to find. Now you must eat."

Vraylok hungrily sampled the fresh fruits, carbo-nitrate casserole and meat pies that Sergon had served while Mahr — ignoring the more substantial fare — nibbled some small lozenges that taste like rock candy laced with mint. Vraylok bit into a succulent pear. "Where do you get summer fruit in the middle of winter?"

"We maintain a greenhouse with artificial climate control that provides fresh produce."

Mahr looked at Vraylok's white teeth and smooth skin. He experienced the nervousness of one who is in the presence of a desirable humanoid. He could think of nothing to say of substance, so commented on Vraylok's apparel.

"I see by the nicks in your travelling boots that you have been long in the crystal storm."

"Yes."

"I myself do not venture out anymore. The memories are too painful." Vraylok swallowed. "But that is why our ancestors created the domes, the crystals, the artificial seasons. So that we would not forget the mistakes of the past."

"Yes, this is a truism." Vraylok patted his lips with a silken napkin and looked at Mahr with sympathy. "One hears a great deal about you, Mahr. That is why I have come. To see if the rumors are true and if I can be of some assistance."

"What rumors are these?"

Vraylok's eyes, flashing like jewels on fire, betrayed his carnal interest. "I hear that you have not given your flesh to another man for over seven orbits. Can this be true?"

"Yes."

"Why?"

"If it were easy to explain, it would be easy to rectify."

"Is it the pressure from your immense responsibilities?"

"There is that. Also there is the burden of my lineage. I am the last of my line and incapable of heterosexual coupling, as are all of the Warrior Women I know."

Vraylok thought about this and smiled. "What would you say were I to offer help?"

Mahr chuckled. "And what can you do to help me?"

Vraylok pushed his plate away and took a sip from the mug of cold ale. "I have traveled a great deal and communicated with many creatures from all parts of the galaxy. I have read widely and have been trained as a scholar. Moreover, I have studied your life and exploits to the degree that I know you better than you might think possible. Including your sexual interests, which my information battery tells me, mesh perfectly with my own."

The artificial winds shifted again and the clicks of the crystals exploding against the window reverberated through the chamber. Shogar awoke, growled a few times and resumed his slumber. Mahr looked at the handsome visitor—the high cheek bones and broad, flat nose—and could no longer ignore the stirring in his body. The heart within that had cried for so long wailed like a siren in his ears. He could no longer feign deafness to the crying of his soul.

125

"I am listening."

"Mahr must heed my words.. The device that creates ever-larger weapons must be destroyed."

"But what of our enemy's weapons?"

"When they learn that you are without, they will come to realize that they no longer have the need."

"And what of our defenses?"

The look of Vraylok's eyes changed from desire to concern. "The defenses must remain. It is your offensive armaments that must be destroyed. Once it is known that you are prepared to defend, but unwilling to attack, the others will follow and dismantle their offensive weaponry. Unnecessary armaments are too costly to maintain."

"My teachers taught me that the best defense is a good offense," argued Mahr.

"That is a myth that began in the arena of sport and wound up on the field of battle. An unfortunate occurrence that changed all of our fates."

"Could so many be so wrong for so many orbits?"

"Apparently. Has the cold war decreased at all since the time of your father? Since the time of your grandfather?"

Mahr eyed Vraylok with a suspicion that was beginning to crumble. Even if he was an emissary from the enemy, he made a lot of sense. "No," admitted Mahr.

"Then perhaps it is time for a different plan." Vraylok placed his slender hand on Mahr's thigh. The ruler shuddered and the warmth of Vraylok's touch caused the last of his doubts to melt.

"If you will permit me," said Vraylok, "I shall pleasure your flesh and feed you the entertainments of my own. I shall walk by your side and help you to keep clear the large issues and small details. As to the continuation of your lineage, I know of Warrior Women who would be pleased to bear your child."

Mahr gazed into Vraylok's eyes and smiled.

"Come," said Vraylok. "Let's walk through the crystal storm. You have, perhaps, forgotten that the crystals melt when close enough to the warmth of a humanoid. We will watch the crystals collide and create fireworks inches from our eyes, then disappear into mist as they touch our skin."

Vraylok ran his fingers through Mahr's silvery hair and lightly massaged the back of his neck. Mahr seized Vraylok about the waist and pressed his bulging musculature to the lithe man's frame. Mahr felt his blood careening through his veins. He hugged Vraylok tightly for a time and then pulled away.

"How do I know that I can trust you?" asked the ruler.

"How do you know that this planet will remain in orbit?"

"It is one of the things in which I must maintain faith."

"And I too."

The ruler stared at the ceramic dream wand, the symbol of power and instrument of war that had been handed down from father to son for millions of time units. Although each man in the chain was aware that it was simply an object of clay, to acknowledge this would be like calling one's father a liar. Whoever held the scepter was supposed to telepathically receive battle plans and ideas for new weapons, but the men of Mahr's family—although never admitting it—knew differently. Like a silly superstition that everyone was afraid to let die, the scepter had allowed the ruling family to retain their position because everyone believed that whoever possessed it held some magical power. Mahr, however, knew that it was just a piece of baked clay with no more significance than a stone in his garden. Would he betray his forefathers and destroy the instrument of aggression that had tyrannized his race for so long?

In his mind's eye, Mahr saw himself seize the dream wand and hurl it to the floor. In his imagination it shatters into a thousand pieces, awakening Shogar. The beast growls and ambles to the debris, sniffing and snarling. Mahr goes to Shogar and smooths his mane, cooing nonsense into his ear. Shogar, breathing easier, salivating less, returns to his corner and gnaws a chunk of rawhide. Sergon appears looking highly distressed, his arms all aflutter about his beefy torso.

"Master, I heard a crashing sound. What happened?"

"Nothing to worry about. Just a pile of broken dreams that must be swept away."

"Master, the dream wand!" The godfather's hands flew to his head, which he shook in disbelief.

"Do not be distressed, Sergon. I will accept the consequences of my act."

For the first time, Mahr realized that he could destroy the dream wand. Once a picture had been created in his mind, the realization was then possible. Someday soon, the cold war would be brought to an end.

Mahr pressed the button on his console that summoned

Sergon. He appeared a few moments later. The ruler draped his arm around Vraylok's shoulder.

"Would you prepare my bedchamber for my guest and myself? We shall return shortly."

"Yes, master."

Sergon scampered out the door. Mahr turned to Vraylok and said, "Come, we shall walk through my garden though winter it still be."

Arm in arm the two men — a Warrior King and a scholar — exited the portals of the massive structure. Artificial sunlight emanating from the dome overhead signalled the dawning of a new rotation. Vraylok cupped his hands and caught the moisture of a thousand melted crystals. He offered the libation to Mahr who thirstily drank his forefathers' bitter tears.

Word Into World

"You are what you read," he said and I readily agreed. I was standing in a bar with some stranger — he looked like he could throw a good cuddle — and he was trying to impress me with the agility of his mind, the dexterity of his tongue.

"Wasn't it Emily Dickinson who said, 'Poetry is language that makes your hair stand on end'?"

"Something like that," I said.

"Well, then the first time I heard real poetry was when I was walking down the street and this alkie bag lady came over and said, 'Be glad I'm not your mother, I would've raised you wrong.' It blew me away."

"I guess it would."

"Then there was the time I was applying for a job, I was completely hard up — debts and bills to pay, nothing in the bank — and I'm desperate for this job and the guy, instead of just saying 'no', delivers this never-ending litany on his philosophy of business, concluding with the sentence, 'So that just goes to show you, you don't fuck with success . . . the job's been filled'. That was poetry, man. Not only did my hair stand up, but my stomach felt like it was juggling half a dozen ball bearings."

He looked at me with expectation but I couldn't think of anything to say so I just sipped my drink and cruised a cute number who looked like he'd never even heard of Emily Dickinson. Tousled brown hair and sneering lips, his tight-as-a-glove bleached jeans had a familiarity and intimacy with his body that I hoped I could attain. But probably never would. Worth a try, though. I struggled to pay attention to the guy I was talking to.

129

"Words, words, words," he said. "Do you know the difference between a word and a world?"

He looked at me like I was supposed to give him a serious answer, but I had no idea what he was talking about.

"The letter l. Get it? Word. World. L."

"Oh."

"Not o — l." He laughed for a while. I glanced at the cutey leaning against the bar.

"And the difference between butch and bitch," I said, "is u and i."

"You and I?" he asked, jabbing his thumb at me and himself.

"No, u and i," I said, drawing the letters in the air between us.

"Oh," he said and laughed.

I excused myself and went to talk to the guy at the bar. He told me right up front how much it would cost. Way beyond my budget. I looked around to find that the guy I'd been talking to was gone.

I went home alone that night and reread all the collected poems of Emily Dickinson. Then I jerked-off and fell asleep.

The Star Of David

"I really felt like I needed a change and just had to see
your reaction." Placing his beer on the bar, he stepped back,
posed, pivoted, and rejoined me. His eyes quizzed my face as
I gulped down the rest of my drink.

"You look fabulous, as usual," I said, "what's the big deal?"

"The problem is that I wanted a different look, and I think
maybe I went too far."

I had heard that line before. Over the years I had seen
Kenny go through his preppy phase which eventually turned
into a flirtation with the jock look. After tiring of that, he had
become a construction worker, a cowboy, and had finally settled into basic clone. Now the mustache, plaid flannel shirt,
and work boots were gone and he sported a red tank top, tight
faded denims, and tennis sneakers. He looked like a suburban
teenager on a Saturday afternoon at the shopping mall.

"You look great in anything, and you know it."

Running his fingers through the thick, brown mane that
framed an affected pout, Kenny shifted his weight and whined,
"Well, I don't know if I should say 'thank you' or 'fuck off'!
Was that a compliment or have I just been read?"

"Take it any way you want—it's your turn to buy the
drinks." I surveyed the crowd while he angled for the bartender's
attention. The kinds of guys that usually came to the Alley
ranged from college-aged pretty boys to mature macho men.
Every major style of dress and attitude mingled freely, and
whether one's tastes were specific or eclectic, Mr. Right For
The Night could easily be found. No wonder the place was always so crowded.

"Here y'are, pardner," Kenny slid into his cowboy drawl,

"let's drink to a fine herd, strong fences, and that good ol' Texas moon."

"You forgot shootin' straight and lovin' hard."

His attention focused on a swarthy bodybuilder with the stance of a bulldog who stood several feet away.

"If you had your gear," I whispered, "you could just lasso the guy and drag him over."

"I was just thinking the same thing." The drawl was gone. "See you later."

I wandered over to the jukebox, checking out the other customers on the way. Reaching into my pocket for some change, I discovered that I had none and was about to return to the bar when someone touched my arm and said, "Excuse me, my name's David, what's yours?"

"Bill."

We exchanged the expected questions, but the words were more than just automatic on my part because this man looked like he'd just stepped out of my fantasies. Suddenly, there were four quarters in my hand. A smile appeared on his face and he said, "Play me some music, okay?"

He placed his hand on my shoulder and gently turned my face toward his own. That incredible smile. His teeth were as perfect and bright as any I'd ever seen, and the lines that formed parentheses around his boysenberry lips were mesmerizing. I inserted the coins in the slot and asked what he liked to listen to.

"Oh, anything." His hand moved down in between my shoulder blades and he rubbed my back in an ever-widening circle. He asked if I'd like another drink, but before I could tell him what I was drinking, he whispered, "I know."

I watched him walk away, quickly pressed some random numbers, and waited for his return. The jeans, faded to a powder blue, stuck to his body like a veneer of paint. The fabric adhered to the two perfectly formed globes in the rear that were joined together like Siamese twins, with a straining seam. In motion, they seemed to sneer defiantly, gracefully propelled by sturdy thighs that pumped rhythmically like the pistons of an engine. His purple t-shirt stretched across hard nipples, and the muscles of his upper arms threatened to sever the sleeves.

I was about to say something, I can't recall just what, when he glared into my eyes as though he could read my mind. The next thing I knew he was holding me, so very tight, that I wanted to melt into his body. I don't think he said anything out loud, and I'm fairly certain I was equally silent, but we moved, as in mutual agreement toward the door and emerged into the balmy warmth of a summer night.

The penthouse apartment had a splendid view of the Hudson River from the high-ceilinged room with wall-to-wall book cases. It seemed like an amazing coincidence at the time because David's library contained every book I could remember reading, plus all those for which I had not yet had the time.

We sat in the living room, he in an overstuffed easy chair, and I on the peach-colored sofa. Between us, an antique mahogany coffee table supported a *TV Guide* ensconced in a Gucci leatherette cover. A state-of-the-art stereo setup and many shelves of records and tapes took up an entire wall. As soon as we'd arrived, he pressed a button and we were surrounded by a Beethoven piano sonata.

"So tell me, Bill," there was that bewitching smile again, "how's your composing coming along?"

"How did you know I'm a composer?"

"I've had my eye on you."

"Are you serious?" I laughed. "I find it very hard to believe that I never noticed *you* before. Do you go to the Alley often?"

"Occasionally, but I travel a lot."

The sonata ended and was succeeded by the sinewy trumpet of Miles Davis. Another favorite. I was really intrigued.

"Yes, Bill, I know what you're thinking. I've been aware of you for some time and asked some questions here and there."

I felt a bit uneasy. The thought of a stranger checking up on me was disturbing, and this man's assured manner and sexy appearance made me a little nervous. He must have sensed it because he came over and sat by my side. Cupping the back of my head with his hand, he pressed his lips to mine and rubbed my stomach. My senses reeled and my cock, fully aroused, strained against my jeans.

"Do you like to play games?" David asked.

I hesitated. "Sometimes."

"What do you think about acting out fantasies?"

"What did you have in mind?"

Leaning over, he playfully bit my neck. "How about a little game of vampire and blood donor?"

I was amused. "You'll be Count Dracula and I'm to play the part of The Victim?"

"Something like that."

"I must confess that I wasn't prepared for this. I left the garlic and wolfsbane at home."

"Perfect."

"Besides, I'm Jewish and don't have a crucifix."

"That's another coincidence," he chuckled, "I'm Jewish too, so a crucifix wouldn't do you any good anyway!" Mimicking the voice and accent of Bela Lugosi, he intoned, "Before de night is over, my pet, you vill find dat ze creatures of de night know everyt'ing about human anatomy. It's a subject dat is very close to our hearts!"

We rose and embraced (such incredible strength) and taking me by the hand, David led me to the bedroom. The indirect crimson lighting gave an eerie quality to the black velvet spread that draped the double bed. White satin-covered pillows were gathered haphazardly by the gleaming brass headboard, and a tiger-skin rug ominously guarded the entrance.

"What, no coffin?"

"There's a layer of native soil between the mattress and box spring."

"I see."

There were no windows. Not even a skylight. I was instructed to undress, get into bed, and pretend I was asleep. He closed the door and left me alone, explaining that he would return momentarily. As I began to disrobe I got the chills. The room seemed to harbor a threatening atmosphere and the cool satin sheets raised goosebumps on my arms. Just as I had found a comfortable position and closed my eyes, he burst through the door, literally tearing it off the hinges. The wooden slab made a dull thud as it hit the floor, and there stood David, naked, breathing heavily. His eyes ablaze, teeth flashing, he slowly made his way to the bed.

"Pretty melodramatic entrance, I'd say. Do you always break down the door when you play this game?"

"You're supposed to be asleep, remember?"

I closed my eyes. I could feel him savagely tear the bedclothes away and an angry snarl leapt from his throat. He lay down on top of me and rubbed his cantilevered, downy chest against my own, skinny and hairless. His arms and legs pinned me, spread-eagle fashion, and his lips and tongue flew about my face, neck, and shoulders. He released my arms and took my cock into his warm, wet mouth. At first it felt like a million tiny feathers tentatively reaching out and teasing me. I started to squirm and he swallowed me whole. I groaned, writhing in a weightless vacuum, my heart beating like a bass drum. I noted, with satisfaction, that I had not once felt his teeth, and finally, unable to hold out any longer, surrendered to the wild spasm that signalled the release of all tension and anxiety. He raised his head and beamed a smile that engulfed me like the blast of warmth from a furnace.

He stroked my thighs, raised my legs and stared into my eyes. My mind suddenly felt like a radio receiver. He seemed to telepathically ask if he could continue.

"Don't stop now," I silently affirmed.

"Message received," he seemed to reply.

His tanned, sculpted torso hovered above as he tenderly, slowly penetrated me. I don't recall that there was any lubrication, but it was blissfully free of pain. He filled me so completely, so snug was the fit that my shriveled cock naturally began to expand and throb again. He played with my nipples and sucked my tongue as he drew himself in and out, massaging my inner being. Every muscle in his arms and chest stood out, taut, as he worked himself into a frenzy. Suddenly, he bit the side of my neck with such intensity that I must have screamed.

He lay down alongside me, our chests rising and falling in perfect harmony. Turning, he smothered me with kisses and drew my tongue into his mouth. For a second, I thought I tasted a hint of blood.

David stood up and sighed, "That was delicious." I began to feel a bit light-headed. My stomach churned audibly. "Are you hungry?"

Before I could answer I was sitting in a high-backed chair at one end of a long table in a room that I hadn't seen before. On the sideboard were several chaffing dishes, a large bowl of greens, and a decanter of white wine. The room was lit entirely by purple candles. David filled a salad bowl, poured a chunky white dressing onto it, and placed it before me.

"Eat!" he commanded. I was in no condition to argue. Skewering a leaf of spinach and a large mushroom with the intricately engraved silver fork which he placed in my hand, I commenced.

"Blue cheese, my favorite. How did you know?" He slowly poured a glass of wine which he set in front of me, and from a different container, fixed himself a large mug of odd looking tomato juice. "Haven't you figured it out yet? I know everything there is to know about you."

"Really?" I mocked, chomping away. "What was the last book I read?"

"*Tar Baby*, by Toni Morrison."

This guy was pretty good. "The last movie I saw?"

"*Raiders Of The Lost Ark.*"

This was getting weird. "What's my brother's name?"

"You don't have a brother. Your sister, whose name is Gayle — with a 'y' — is twenty-eight, and the weekday afternoon dj at WLAC in San Diego . . . would you like some more salad?"

"Are you clairvoyant?"

"Would you like me to tell you what you're thinking right now?"

"Sure, fill me in."

"Aside from your obvious bewilderment about my mind reading abilities, you had just flashed on the title of William Burroughs' *Naked Lunch* because you've never eaten a meal without your clothes on before."

He stalked over to the sideboard, every muscle defined, the candles casting taffeta patterns on his smooth skin. He deftly tossed noodles, cream, butter, cheese, pepper, and parsley. A generous portion was placed before me.

"Okay, Mr. Wizard, would you like to tell me what's going on?"

"I'll talk if you'll eat."

"Aren't you eating anything?"

"I rarely eat solids these days, bad for my digestion." I twirled some fettucini on the fork and brought it to my mouth. "Bill," he said seriously, "I have powers that you will never be able to understand. Look at the salt shaker."

I glanced at the small crystal container. It rocked back and forth for a few seconds and became a small frog that jumped off the table. In mid-air it changed into a screeching bat that circled my head, then settled on the table, right next to the pepper, turning back into a salt shaker.

"Did you put acid in the salad dressing or are you some kind of hypnotist?"

"Neither. I am unlike anyone — and anything — you have ever met before. I have, er, special abilities." The lazy speech pattern was gone. The tone had become clipped, imperious; the accent, Eastern European.

"You're as good with dialects as my friend, Kenny."

"Oh yes, Kenny. Cute kid, but fickle." He paused. "My name is David Ben Zvi. I am over eight-hundred-years-old and come from a place that has long been forgotten. I belong to a secret cult which dotes on young males who happen to be gay — Jewish virgins. SILENCE! You were about to inform me that you were not a virgin. When I use that word I am speaking of those whose jugulars have not previously been defiled. Remember when I bit your neck? I nearly drained you. That is why I had some nourishment prepared."

I was beginning to doubt my sanity. Or his. He sipped his drink. "It is not tomato juice. It is blood. Human. Delectable. To continue, I can read your every thought and can place images in your mind. You see me as young and attractive. I am, however, quite old and unpleasant to look at. I believe the word 'troll' is the current popular description."

It was not easy to believe that this gorgeous stud was what he claimed.

"You will fall asleep in my bed tonight, but you will awaken in your own apartment. You will remember everything."

I was not convinced but decided to play along. "Won't I become a vampire?"

"Hardly . . . you have seen too many bad movies."

"Will I ever see you again?"

"No. You are no longer a virgin."

"So, how about if we skip the transfusion and just have sex? You were wonderful."

"I am afraid that is not possible. Having forfeited your status as virgin, you are no longer attractive to me. But I will protect you from the fangs of others. Now that I have had you it is my wish that no one else shall ever drink from your jugular again. When you awaken you will be in possession of a small amulet of protection which will be invisible to all mortals, except yourself. It is my gift in exchange for the exquisite taste of your blood."

I decided this guy was a terrific actor. There was probably some acid or mescaline in the food. He was probably a professional mesmerist, as well.

He led me back to the bedroom, the door having been miraculously restored to its hinges. We clung together in the dark until he rolled away and began to snore. I slipped into a deep slumber and had a terrifying dream.

137

David and I ran down a long stretch of beach; the ocean, a clear turquoise. We stopped to catch our breath and, confident that we had escaped our pursuers, sat down to rest. After a prolonged necking session, he went for a swim while I stretched out in the sand, the sun painting my skin a reddish brown. Suddenly, I felt two powerful hands circle my neck. I opened my eyes to find a huge salivating creature with rancid breath bearing down on me. I yelled for David as the hands grew tighter around my throat. I choked, gasping for air, then woke up.

I was in my bedroom. There was the poster from the 1967 World's Fair on the far wall. My bookshelf, crammed from top to bottom with music scores and dog-eared paperbacks stood near the bed and my clock-radio, old faithful, sat silently on the night table, the second hand slowly making the usual rounds.

My neck felt strange. As if someone or something had been trying to strangle me. I raised my hand to feel the skin and touched a metallic chain. I do not own any jewelry. Never have.

I ran to the bathroom, switched on the light and looked in the mirror. A small six-pointed star, suspended on a fine chain, dangled in the hollow of my throat. A closer examination revealed six tiny amethysts, one at the apex of each point. I blinked in disbelief. Working my hands around the chain I discovered that it did not have a clasp. I tested its strength. It would not break. I was still admiring the way it lay against my skin when the telephone rang.

"Good morning, Bill. I hope you had as good a time last night as I did."

"Kenny," I had to clear my throat, "I have to show you something and tell you a story that you will not believe. But you must!"

"How about brunch? Peter's Pavilion in about an hour?"

I showered and shaved, faster than I ever had before. I wanted to arrive at the restaurant before Kenny so I could see his reaction when he noticed the star.

He didn't. I sat, head held high, trying to show off my new acquisition. He immediately started to rattle off all the sordid details of his night with the bodybuilder. I listened patiently, craning my neck, but he did not notice.

". . . and then we woke up and did it again. Can you believe it?"

I sipped my coffee. "Kenneth! Will you please stop for a second and say something nice about my star?"

"Huh?"

I grasped it between my thumb and pointer.

"The only thing I see on your neck is the biggest hickey ever. What did you go home with last night, a rattlesnake?"

I told him everything I could remember about David, his apartment, and all of the bizarre things that had happened. I had no appetite whatsoever and my eggs Benedict remained untouched. Kenny shoveled his into his mouth like a fireman stoking a steam locomotive.

"If I were you, dear," he swallowed the last of it, "I'd cut down on the booze and poppers . . . anyway, to change the subject, I was thinking of getting one of those spiky haircuts, like the New Wave rock stars. What do you think about a streak of green, right here on the side?"

"You'll never be satisfied with the way you look," I said, exasperated.

"At least my reputation as the Chameleon of the West Village will be intact."

After paying the bill, we strolled to the pier. I found myself constantly checking the star. I touched it. Ran my fingers around the chain. I was certain that it was there.

Two years and four months later, on a freezing December night, I walked down Christopher Street bundled up with gloves, ear muffs, and a scarf. No one had acknowledged my star and I never mentioned it to anyone, fearing that I would be labelled crazy. I noticed a figure walking toward me. In the distance I could not make out his features, but as he drew closer I could see that he was just my type. He walked right over and introduced himself. We chatted for a minute or two, but it was far too cold to talk on the street so I invited him to my apartment.

"Make yourself comfortable."

"Nice place." He walked over to the piano and played a few chords. I removed my scarf just as he turned to look at me. He stared at my throat and scowled. Shrinking away, breathing deeply, he screamed something in a language I could not identify. He pointed at my neck and backed toward the door. Turning, he grasped the doorknob with both hands and yanked it off. Still screaming, he hurled it to the floor, and with both fists, pounded on the door until the entire frame splintered noisily apart and crashed out into the hall. He ran down the stairs faster than I had ever seen anyone move.

Getting my door repaired proved to be one of the major hassles of my life. Gayle flew in from the coast to help me stand guard until my apartment was secure. It took three days. We both drank lots of coffee, took turns sleeping, and ate countless chocolate bars. The story I told her to explain my predicament did not contain one shred of truth and she had no trouble believing it.

When I told Kenny (hair shaved off, black leather and studs from head to toe) what really happened, he laughed at me. But I can still feel the star and chain, and mirrors confirm its presence. At least, to me.

Body Language

Looking down at the dry stain on the blanket, Roger remembered spitting out the semen and saliva after Charlie came in his mouth. Recalling the foul taste, he handled the blanket at arm's length, as though it were diseased. Folding it, making sure that his fingers did not touch the soiled part, he tucked it into his laundry bag.

Roger had planned to suck Charlie's cock. All of the gestures and signs he had developed to attract attention to his own cock were sublimated so that the focus would be on Charlie's. The message was obvious, the language — though silent — clear and direct: I want to suck your cock. Tease it, devour it, feel it grow.

The pleasure would be mutual. Roger would enjoy making Charlie writhe and groan, as Charlie would revel in feeling his cock harden, the nerve endings stroked until almost numb, the tension and release of a satisfying orgasm. But Charlie tried to take what Roger wanted to give, and a gift is robbed of all meaning if it's stolen.

Charlie had not understood, was unable to distinguish between two acts which look similar but are completely different. Cocksucking may look like facefucking, but anyone who's tried either knows that they have little in common. A cocksucker takes the active role by manipulating his partner, who remains passive. A facefucker ignores the artistry of the cocksucker by thrusting his cock into the mouth and throat as though it were merely a convenient orifice with nothing special to offer.

Roger and Charlie had knelt on the bed, face to face. Bending, Roger embraced Charlie's cock with his lips. He provided saliva, worked his tongue, created vacuums, caressed with his cheeks and palate. Charlie responded by seizing Roger's hair.

He rammed his cock into Roger's mouth. Forcing him to lie down on his back, Charlie straddled his head and pumped his face like a jackhammer.

Roger did not resist. He could not bring himself to deny Charlie the pleasure of an orgasm, even though he suddenly found himself not enjoying what had, a few moments before, been sublime.

To explain the difference between giving and taking, sucking and being fucked would destroy any vestige of propriety, mystery, sensuality. The sperm, which would have tasted pungent and creamy was rendered bitter, slimy. The mouthful that Roger had planned on savoring and swallowing was instantly spat onto the blanket in disgust.

Roger locked the door and slung the laundry bag over his shoulder. Leaving the building, walking up the street, he could still recall the awful taste on his tongue. He exchanged the bag for a ticket at the launderer's, wishing he could erase the memory from his mind as easily as stains can be removed from blankets.

Telesex

"Good morning, Harry, this is Computer Central. Here is what you have to look forward to today: at 10:00 the paintings you wanted framed will be delivered; at 12:00 noon you have a luncheon appointment at Venus' with Joan; at 3:00 you have a Telesex date with #4017; and at 10:00 this evening you and Frank are expected at Eugene's party. It will be warm and sunny all day with temperatures in the seventies, and this evening will be pleasant with the temperature going down to sixty-five. Have a nice day."

Pressing the button that raises the metallic window shades, Harry turned and looked at Frank. Blond and brawny, he lay fast asleep as the morning sun filtered into the room. Harry waited a few seconds to see if Frank would respond to the warm massage of the solar rays, but his dreaming and steady breathing went undisturbed.

Harry pressed the Fuzak button before sauntering over to the bathroom, and the sound of synthesized polyrhythms gently permeated the three-room apartment. The bathroom light switched on automatically upon entrance. Harry slowly examined his body in the full-length mirror and smiled, grateful that he could maintain his trim physique without ever thinking about diet or exercise.

His hips kept time with the electro-pulse during the soaping, rinsing, and toweling dry. He switched on the sunlamp and, after exposing himself for a few micro-seconds longer than necessary, strapped the U-test-it onto his arm. His heart beat faster and his breathing quickened until the needle pointed to "normal."

He entered the bedroom to find Frank, awake now with headset and goggles in place, stroking himself vigorously. Harry walked over to Frank's terminal and picked up the cassette case: *Chet Fucks Luke In The Barn*. He grimaced. Making a mental note to pick up some new cassettes, he pressed the breakfast button. Moments later Frank came, moaning and sighing. He removed the headset and goggles and watched Harry zipping up his electric blue leisure pants.

"Good morning, handsome," said Frank, wiping himself off.

Harry walked over to the bed and kissed him on the forehead.

"Breakfast will be ready in about ten minutes."

As Frank headed towards the bathroom, Harry noted that the well-developed body he had fallen in love with was now doughy flab. Picking up the *Chet Fucks Luke In The Barn* cassette, he ripped out the Vi-cel, broke the plastic in two, and dumped the remains in the garbage receptacle.

The radio in the kitchen was tuned to the all-talk station, and discussion centered on whether a thirty-year-old rhythm and blues star could be taken seriously as a presidential contender. Harry buttered an English muffin and reached for the jam jar.

"So, who are you doing today?"

"Well," yawned Frank, "Mrs. Vanderkamp is coming in at eleven. She's a total bitch, but her hair is easy and she always has terrific gossip. Early this afternoon Peter Stone is coming in. He made a special request *pour moi!*"

"No shit? Tell him your lover adores his Fruit-Of-The-Loom ads. Especially the one where all he has on is the white briefs with the hard-hat and work boots. Hot stuff!"

Frank reached for a second helping of scrambled eggs. Harry swallowed the last of his muffin and scowled.

"Must you have more? You're turning into a real pig."

"I always have seconds."

"Yeah, but you used to work it off."

Frank's cheeks reddened.

"I used to have a good reason to work out. I didn't mind the sweat and strain because I wanted to look good. For you."

He stood up and threw down his napkin.

"If you ever decide to kiss on the lips and have sex without Fucksuits or computers, I'll rejoin the gym."

He grabbed his yellow windbreaker and left the apartment, cursing the sliding door panel that closed quietly no matter how hard you pressed the button.

☆ ☆ ☆

144

Joan, in a white crepe de chine blouse, purple spandex slacks and patent leather heels was already seated at the table when Harry arrived.

"Am I late?"

"No, I was early and couldn't stand the thought of sitting at the bar."

Harry surveyed the view of Central Park, told Joan how well she looked, and signalled the waiter.

"I'd like a bourbon and water . . . ready for another?"

"Absolutely!"

"And another for the lady . . . so, how're things at the shop?"

"Not quite the same since you became a millionaire and quit."

"Is it my fault the old man had the King Midas touch and died so young?"

"No, of course not. But just because you don't *have* to work doesn't mean you should just sit around all the time doing nothing. You must really be bored."

"I am," he admitted.

"So, take up a hobby. Do volunteer work. Write a book, take a course, weave baskets, but do *something!*"

"I'm still getting used to the idea of being alive."

The slim waiter with Tenaxed black hair appeared with the drinks.

"How much longer are you going to use that as an excuse? The scare is over and you, like countless others, survived."

"I know . . . it's just that I'm still terrified. I thought I would be dead by now."

"But you're not. And the crisis is over."

She paused and watched him sip his cocktail. "How's Frank?"

Harry sighed.

"We had another fight this morning. It was my fault but I couldn't help it."

"You're too much. Let me remind you that he stuck by your side through the entire ordeal. He *loves* you. You shouldn't be so hard on him."

Joan checked her lipstick in the mirror of her compact and closed it slowly as the waiter returned and handed them menus.

"The soup of the day is gazpacho and the vegetables are broccoli and summer squash. I'll be back in a few minutes to take your order."

Harry tried to alter the course of the conversation. "So, what do you think about Michael Jackson running for president?"

Joan sipped her sherry.

"If a lousy actor can be president, then why not a great singer? But anyway, getting back to the subject, the doctor says you're fine, the Center For Disease Control has declared the emergency over, no doubt you tested your blood this morning and it's normal . . ." Harry looked away, embarrassed, ". . . so what are you so afraid of?"

He gulped the last of his drink.

"Dying."

"You're going to die someday whether you like it or not and sex will probably have nothing to do with it."

Avoiding her penetrating hazel eyes he picked up the menu. "I'm starved. What looks good to you?"

"You are one helluva lucky motherfucker. You get cured of a strange disease and turn around to find yourself suddenly rich. You live with a good man who loves you. Get over yourself, darling, and start living again. It'll be a lot easier on all of us."

"The only reason the old man left me anything at all was because he thought I'd never live to claim it! He never gave me a dime when I needed money for treatments."

"I guess you showed him, huh?"

Harry, defeated, avoided her gaze.

"I think I'll have the gazpacho and lobster tails . . . how about you?"

Joan stopped playing with the ends of her long, straight hair and, flipping the strands over her shoulder, glanced out the window.

"I'm not that hungry. I think I'll just have a salad or something."

☆ ☆ ☆

The pink and magenta Mini-rob rolled over to Frank's chair on command.

"Ms. Simpson would like some coffee, please."

"How would you like it?" asked the soothing, androgynous voice of the mechanical slave.

"With just a touch of cream, as usual."

A white styrofoam cup with steaming coffee materialized as a side panel slid open and a metallic tentacle slowly pro-

146

pelled it toward Ms. Simpson's outstretched hand. Her chalky cheeks cracked revealing a tentative smile.

"Thank you, dear," she said to the machine.

"You're quite welcome," it replied.

"Rollers and clips," said Frank.

The Mini-rob repositioned itself by the stylist's side and a platform bearing the requested objects rose from the top of the mechanism until it was within reach. Frank started brushing and separating the wavy strands of pimento-colored hair.

"I want to know everything," said the aging spinster. Frank nimbly clipped a roller into place.

"I did Mrs. Vanderkamp this morning and she's positively certain that Brooke and Mick are going to separate and divorce . . . and *he's* taking custody of the child. Could you just die?"

"I knew it would never last. I was just saying to Ernestine the other day that it was the most unlikely thing to happen since Streisand agreed to a concert tour to raise money for AIDS research."

Frank, who had never really liked the singer until she generously donated her talent to the fund-raising drive, had gone out and purchased all of her records. The Beatles had always been his favorites, but he began to hum "People" under his breath.

"Frank," said Ms. Simpson between sips, "I happen to know that you did Peter Stone, just a few hours ago, and I want to know what he's like."

Spraying a clump of hair with the atomizer that hung from his utility belt, he cleared his throat.

"What, exactly, would you like to know?"

"I've heard that he is as stupid as he is handsome."

Frank suppressed a wicked grin. "He's not what you would call an intellectual, but he's a nice person, definitely not spoiled by his success."

"And his next project?"

"He just signed to do the magazine campaign for the new line of Club Baths jockstraps."

The mere thought caused a sensation in Frank's crotch. He excused himself, walked to the reception area and absently looked at his schedule. He returned when the swelling had begun to subside. Observing his approach, his client remarked, "My dear, you really are putting on a lot of weight. You used to look so athletic."

"One of these days I'm going to start working out again
. . . I've just been too busy lately."

Ms. Simpson eyed him suspiciously.

"And how is Harry these days?"

"Oh, he's just fine."

"Are you two getting along any better these days?"

"Oh, yes . . . everything's terrific . . . would you like some
more coffee?"

"No, thank you, I think I've had quite enough!"

☆ ☆ ☆

Harry looked up at the monorail above as he walked downtown. He had sent the chauffeur and limo home, wanting to
take the opportunity to walk and think. Computer Central had,
as usual, been correct. The sky was cloudless, the sun strong,
and a gentle breeze played with his hair. En route he purchased
a new copy of *Chet Fucks Luke In The Barn*, and also picked
up a new cassette for Frank's collection.

Entering the apartment, he paused to admire the paintings in their new frames and proceeded to the bedroom. He
stripped and fetched the bulky Telesex uniform from the closet,
zippered himself into it, and sat down on the bed. He donned
his headset and goggles, plugged the suit into the computer,
and switched on his terminal.

"Ready!"

"Good afternoon, Harry. You will make contact in exactly
one minute and eleven seconds."

He lay down and started to think about #4017. The blond
hair, finely honed torso, massive arms and thighs and meaty
buns reminded him of the way Frank looked several years before. And soon, hunky #4017 would be his. Sort of. With their
touch-sensitive suits on and the audio and video strictly con-
trolled, it would almost be like real sex, with no danger of actual contact. He had examined the catalog very carefully and
was thrilled when #4017 had agreed to a Telesex date.

Suddenly a test pattern appeared before his eyes and a
low hum entered his ears. Moments later the computer spoke.

"Many apologies, Harry. I am sorry to tell you that we
have a malfunctioning computer chip in our circuits. This date
must be postponed until full repairs can be made."

"Shitfuck! Are you sure?"

"Yes. There is no way to circumvent it. Many apologies.
An appointment with a repairman is being made at this very
moment."

148

Harry tore off the headset and goggles and practically ripped the Telesex uniform from his body. He flung it against the wall, stormed into the living room, and poured himself a bourbon at the chrome and lucite bar. He quickly gulped two shots of the stuff and poured himself a third, to sip. Unwrapping a new pack of Columbian cannabis cigarettes, he lit one and inhaled deeply.

☆ ☆ ☆

When Frank arrived home he slipped into the apartment and discovered Harry in the kitchen. Cleaning and chopping vegetables, casual in cut-offs and a tank-top, the running water prevented him from hearing Frank's entrance. Frank snuck up behind him, gathered him in his arms, and kissed him on the back of the neck.

"I was gonna suggest that we call out for Japanese/Cuban, but I see you have something else in mind."

"I got stoned and turned on the video and there was one of those cooking shows on and I realized I hadn't done any cooking in at least a century so I went out and bought some things and here I am." He flicked a piece of cucumber rind off his thumb and returned to his task. "Dinner will be in about a half-hour, okay?"

Frank walked past the newly framed paintings without even noticing their presence. He entered the living room, fixed himself a scotch, and drank it slowly while listening to a Beatles tape.

They sat at the kitchen table and ate by candlelight while the electro-pulse kept time in the background.

"This is the best tarragon chicken ever," said Frank, wiping his mouth with a mauve cloth napkin.

"Thanks . . . actually it's pretty easy."

"Ah, but the seasoning is so subtle, so perfect."

"Would you like some more?" asked Harry with a smile, hoping the offer would compensate for his attitude at breakfast.

"No thanks." Frank looked down at the belly that hung out over his belt. "It's really terrific, but I've got to start doing something about all of this excess baggage I've been carting around. You know, this is the first meal created by human hands in this apartment since before your illness."

"Yeah, I figured it was time to start getting back into things." He paused and stared into Frank's blue eyes. "I've sort

149

of been toying with the idea of going back to work. Joan said I could probably get my old job back at Cartier's."

"That's the best news I've heard all day."

"Are you sure you wouldn't like some more?"

Frank shook his head.

"Can I help with the dishes?"

"Nope. I'm just gonna toss this stuff into the Steri-unit and deal with the rest tomorrow. We have a party to go to."

While Frank headed for the living room, Harry collected all of the dirty dishes and utensils. He knew that Frank would want to sit and digest for a while, and then go to the bedroom for his usual post-dinner yank session. Harry got the new cassette from the closet and handed it to Frank.

"Honey, while I was out today I picked up a little something for you."

He watched as the crimson ribbons and floral paper were slowly undone.

"*Tom The Sailor Strips and Poses!* I've always wanted this one. How did you know?"

Frank stood up and gave Harry a long hug.

Harry whispered, "I was wondering if you felt like, uh, you know, fooling around? We've still got two hours before we have to leave."

"Certainement, mon cheri. I must visit le pissoir, see you in le boudoir," he winked.

Harry sat naked on the bed, nervously rubbing his palms together when Frank entered. Sheathed from neck to wrists and ankles in a sheer latex body condom, he clutched another in his hand. Harry rose, took the Fucksuit, and tossed it in the corner. Grabbing the back of Frank's neck, he brought their mouths together and touched his lover's tongue with his own. He stepped back, smiling, and peeled the hygienic garment from Frank's body. Guiding him to the bed, he lay down and pulled Frank down alongside. He rolled on top of him and gently kissed the parted lips of the man he loved.

BOOKS FROM BANNED BOOKS

Ripening,
Valerie Taylor $8.95
Profiles Encourage (Nonfiction),
Pamela S. Johnson $8.95
Like Coming Home: Coming-Out Letters (Nonfiction),
Edited by Meg Umans $7.95
A Herd of Tiny Elephants,
Stan Leventhal $8.95
Dairy of a New York Queen,
William Barber $8.95
gay(s)language,
H. Max $4.95
Kite Music,
Gary Shellhart $8.95
Mountain Climbing in Sheridan Square,
Stan Leventhal $8.95
Skiptrace,
Antoinette Azolakov $8.95
A Cry in the Desert,
Jed A. Bryan $9.95
Cass and the Stone Butch,
Antoinette Azolakov $8.95
Dreams of the Woman Who Loved Sex,
Tee Corinne $7.95
Tangled Sheets,
Gerard Curry $7.95
Death Strip,
Benita Kirkland $8.95
Days in the Sun,
Drew Kent $8.95
Fairy Tales Mother Never Told You,
Benjamin Eakin $5.95
The Gay of Cooking Cookbook,
The Kitchen Fairy $10.95

These books are available from your favorite bookstore or by mail from:

BANNED BOOKS
Number 231, P.O. Box 33280, Austin, Texas 78764

Add $1.50 postage and handling for one (1) book. For more than one book, add 10% of order total. Texas residents, please also add 8% sales tax. Send your name and address for our free current catalog and to be added to our mailing list.